NINETY-NINE REASONS

NINETY-NINE REASONS

Elisheba Haxby
& Jesse Vincent

Above The Sun
Publishing

Printed in the United States of America

ISBN-13: 978-1-7336006-0-6

Published by Above The Sun,
Eugene, Oregon

Cover by Deranged Doctor Designs

For Daniel

June 14, 9:11 p.m. – Tamara

Images from last night's nightmare clung to my mind as I stepped out of the shower. Ryan's body looming over me, features mangled by the intensity of his hatred and need for revenge. There was no mercy in his eyes. Fear crept down my spine and slithered its way into my stomach. With shaky hands, I wrapped a towel around myself and slid down the wall.

I closed my eyes and pressed my head into my knees, trying to shake the terrible thoughts. His fingers around my neck, squeezing the life out of me. No one there to hear my useless screams.

I drew in a slow breath, to calm my racing heart. The dream hadn't faded like it was supposed to. Even at work today, the gruesome scene had been stuck on repeat. In some ways, though, I was thankful. This dream had kept me two steps ahead of Ryan for the past three and a half years. Now it was ushering me forward once again. My gut wrenched—equal parts fear and sadness. My time in Ocean Shores was coming to an end.

I had to leave before he found me.

Taking in a deep breath, I pushed myself up off the bathroom floor, walked into my bedroom, and dressed in a floral baby-doll shirt, skinny jeans, and tennis shoes.

I tidied up the small room, then gathered the wad of cash from my purse. I flipped up the gray and white comforter draped over my bed and reached around the stack of novels for the wine jug. Three weeks ago, when the nightmare first started again, I purchased a gallon jug of wine, dumped out the contents, and started an escape fund. Somewhat wasteful, I know, but the design seemed perfect for a savings jar. The narrow top made it hard to fish out of. I shoved in the forty-six dollars in tips I had made today at Bennett's Fish Shack. That should make about three hundred dollars. At this rate, it would take months to leave. Maybe I needed to find a second job. I grabbed the Camel 99s from my purse, tapped one out of the box, and stared dejectedly at the money jar. I lit up and breathed in a long drag.

Nothing in me wanted to leave. It was peaceful here. Some days, the beauty of this place made it easy to forget that other life I came from. Walks on the beach cleansed my soul. In those moments, I could pretend I hadn't made the mistakes that brought me here. When I first drove into town, a little less than a year ago, it felt like coming home. For someone like me, who'd been on the run since … well, as long as I can remember, finding a home was an undeserved gift.

I took another drag. I wanted to stay, but I needed to go. My phone dinged, interrupting my thoughts.

`Where are you?`

My best friend, Shelby Turner. I inhaled a pull from my cigarette and blew out the smoke. How would I ever say goodbye to Shelby? Though I'd been here less than a year, in so many ways, she had become my sister. My stomach twisted sharply. Sister … Truth was, I didn't deserve a sister after I had abandoned mine.

The phone dinged again.

`I thought you'd be here by now.`

We were supposed to be meeting up tonight at our favorite hangout, Midway's Pub. I had told her I'd meet her at 9:30. It wasn't even 9:15, but that was Shelby.

Patience was *not* a virtue she possessed.

I glanced in the mirror and ran a hand through my damp hair. If Shelby wasn't already impatiently waiting, I might have blown it out to give it a bit more body. Instead, I scrunched it a few times and then dabbed mascara on my lashes. Shelby would no doubt scold me for not taking more time on my appearance, but there was nobody in Ocean Shores I wanted to impress. I donned my jacket and headed out the door.

Thoughts of Ryan engulfed me again as I secured the lock. I swallowed the fear rising in my throat. I had prayed a thousand times that he would give up looking, but prayer hadn't done much for me before. He would never stop.

Outside, the air was damp, and a cool breeze blew across my face. The familiar ocean scent calmed my nerves a bit.

My phone dinged again as I put my key in the door of my '85 Volkswagen Cabriolet.

`Are you close? I just took my third shot.`

Oh, boy. It's gonna be one of those nights.

`On my way.`

It only took a minute and a half to reach Midway's. Walking would have taken a mere eight minutes, and if I had planned to drink tonight, that's what I would have done. But I didn't drink much anymore. The only thing alcohol had ever done for me was give me hangovers and regret.

My friends, Caiden and Milly, stood outside the door, smoking and chatting. Caiden was tall and lanky with thin lips and a birdlike, beaky nose. Milly had short, wispy blonde hair that framed her delicate features.

"Hey, Tamara," Milly called out. "Come have a smoke with us. Caiden has got quite the story for you."

"Can't. Shelby's been blowing up my phone."

Caiden smirked and raised his hands in a playful gesture. "Nuff said. We'll catch up later."

I nodded and walked through the door, flashing my fake ID. Shelby had scored them for us a few months ago, since neither of us were of drinking age quite yet. Only six more months to go.

The familiar smell of stale beer and cheap cologne hung in the air. I scanned the half-full bar for Shelby. Open-Mic Friday always drew a decent crowd. Carla, one of Ocean Shores' favorite local artists, was on stage singing a cover of "Cowboy, Take Me Away." Her big Eighties hairdo bounced around as she swayed to the music she sang.

Off to the left were two pool tables. A guy with a tattoo sleeve was queuing up to take a shot.

Shelby came out of nowhere and threw her arms around me. "There you are, chica! I thought you'd never come." Her blonde hair didn't have a lock out of place, and her makeup was done to perfection, accenting her big blue eyes, high cheekbones, and full lips. She wore a blue sequined top and a black miniskirt that flaunted her Marilyn Monroe curves. "Are you ready for a shot? I just had another double." She pulled me toward the bar and waved Charlie down.

"I'm thinking I'll start off slow."

"Hey, Tamara." Charlie smiled and a little dimple appeared on his chin. He was one of the best-looking gingers I'd ever seen. And his good-hearted personality made him even more attractive. "What can I get you this fine evening?"

If I ever did decide to date, Charlie would have been my first choice. Last fall, when I first met him at a party, he had seemed interested in me, but then Shelby swooped in with her normal exuberant flirtation. He chose her that night, and their month-long whirlwind romance ended in a train wreck. Because of that, he was off the table, but that was fine because I didn't date, anyway.

"She'll take a Jager Bomb to start," Shelby piped in before I had a chance to respond. "My girl needs to catch up with me." There was a slight slur in her voice.

Charlie's eyebrow shot up. "Jager Bomb? I thought you were more of a Cosmo or Lemon Drop kind of girl?"

I smirked. If he knew my drink choices, maybe I *did* come in too much. Thoughts of my savings jar ran through my mind. Wasting money on drinks was a bad idea. Beer was probably the cheapest option, and I could sip it slowly throughout the night. "How 'bout a Coors Light and two glasses of water?"

Shelby rolled her eyes. "You're no fun sometimes."

I stuck my tongue out at her, and we both laughed. "I don't need alcohol to be fun."

"True, but it doesn't hurt." She flashed a goofy smile, but then looked past me to the stage. "Oh, my, my. Who is that?"

I turned and followed her gaze. A guy was walking to the center of the stage, a guitar slung over his chest. He was around six feet tall with a lean, muscular build. His features were defined and, well, beautiful. He reminded me a bit of Jared Leto when he was younger, before he went emo.

The announcer's voice came over the speakers. "Ladies and gentlemen, we have some new blood tonight, coming all the way from Redding, California. Give it up for Danny McMillan."

Shelby leaned in. "He's super-hot. Let's get a closer look." She jumped up off her barstool, grabbed me by the hand, and pulled me forward.

"Hello, Ocean Shores. I've been in this town for three short days." He had a slight New York accent when he spoke.

Hadn't the announcer said he was from Redding?

"The first night I was here, I had a dream about a beautiful angel girl with dark hair and emerald green eyes." Danny paused, and swept back his dark, chin-length hair.

"Sounds like you," Shelby whispered in my ear as we made our way through the crowd.

"Yeah, right." Inwardly, though, there was a jolt to my core.

"She had been through some hard things in life and needed someone to love her." Danny cleared his throat. "The storms of life had broken her wings, but when our worlds collided, she was still strong enough to save me."

The first part of that did sound like me, but I'd never be strong enough to save someone else. I could barely save myself.

"Lately, I've been going through some hard things, but this dream made me feel like maybe God was about to answer some of my prayers. When I woke up, there was a melody in my heart, and all I could think about was this girl."

Talking about God and answered prayers at a bar felt out of place. Yet, there was something poetic and poignant in his words, as if he was speaking from his heart.

"I haven't met her yet." He put his hand in his pocket and pulled out a pick. "If anybody knows her, send her my way. I wrote this song for her."

Shelby nudged me again. I glanced at her, and she wiggled her eyebrows.

I rolled my eyes.

Danny strummed the guitar, and the beautiful melody washed over me.

"Trucker dropped you off in some one-horse town
As the day becomes the night.
All alone and nowhere to go
And frankly, barely alive."

Something in me stirred. Images of the first time I had to run filled my vision. It was almost as if this stranger on the stage had seen into my world and written my life into a song.

"Baby, God's got a plan and a strong young man
He made for you before you were born.
He's on his way through the wind
and the rain to take you home."

The words struck my soul in a strange way, and tears immediately stung the back of my eyes. God's got a plan? Was that even possible after everything? The idea seemed foreign but … inviting. In so many ways, I was only half-living after everything I had been through.

Swallowing hard, I pushed the emotion away and focused my attention on the man onstage. His dark hair kept falling over his face as he strummed. His voice carried such depth and passion that his lone presence took over the whole stage.

"He's got a place on the hill overlooking
some things he calls paradise.
It's a little home at the end of the road
Where you'll spend the rest of your life.
So, don't close your eyes, don't lay down and die,
'cause, baby, that fate's not for you.
You got sixty years of laughter and tears
And you got work left in this world."

Longing blossomed inside my chest. One of my deepest desires was to be in a stable place where I didn't have to run anymore. A dangerous desire. One I never let myself fantasize about. One I kept locked up deep inside. One that, most the time, I fooled myself into believing didn't matter.

"Somebody's gonna love you, carry you back home.
To hell with the rain. It's a magical day.
It's a done deal. It's written down in stone.
So, go, baby, go, baby, go, baby, go.
Don't close your eyes.
You're a heartbeat away, just south of paradise."

For a moment, it seemed like he was looking at me, singing directly to me. The feeling in my chest intensified, as if a breaker that had been blown years ago had finally been switched back on, and I was all sorts of lit up.

Somebody's gonna love you ... Such simple, yet endearing words. That was an even deeper longing than having a place to call home. Tears threatened to come again. What was wrong with me? I couldn't listen to another word without falling apart.

"I'm going to go smoke," I told Shelby and then, before she could protest, I bolted out the door at the back of the bar.

June 14, 10:02 p.m. – Tamara

I lit up and paced, sucking in a thoughtful drag. What was that about? Maybe it was because I'd already been sad about leaving Ocean Shores.

Somebody's gonna love you …

Those words struck an infinitely lonely chord inside my heart. And the fact that the song was about a woman on the run—

Stop it, Tamara. Don't do this to yourself.

A light wind blew across my face. Taking another pull from my cigarette, I allowed myself to think about him on the stage and the way he sang—like he lived and breathed the words of the song and then exhaled them, giving them life. Though it was somewhat chilly outside, heat crept up my neck.

Maybe I should just leave town tonight. I flicked the ash off my smoke and took another drag, continuing to pace.

No. I didn't have enough money to leave yet.

I wouldn't let some sexy stranger with a powerful voice and soul-piercing lyrics scare me out of town. For all I knew, he was just passing through. With his talent and looks, he was probably on his way to Hollywood or Nashville. Ocean Shores was for people more like me. People who didn't want to be noticed—or found.

"That bad, huh?" Charlie's voice startled me. The door closed behind him, and he chucked a bag of trash in the Dumpster next to me.

I looked up, my eyes questioning. "What are you talking about?" I flicked my cigarette onto the ground and stomped on it. "The singer?"

"Yeah. Just so you know, he's asking around about you."

My heart jolted. Why would he ask about me?

"Don't worry, Shelby is distracting him."

"He's with Shelby?" The tone in my voice had a ring of alarm.

"It's cool." He grabbed an empty box by the Dumpster. "I already warned him about her." He stepped on the box, breaking it down.

"Wait, you know him?"

"He's my cousin." He smashed another box with his foot. "He's staying out on some family property for a while to get his head straight."

"His head straight? From what?" I pulled a cigarette out of my pack and offered it to him.

He eyed the cigarette in my hand and then shook his head. "That's his story to tell."

"Sorry. I shouldn't have asked." Inwardly, I chided myself for being so nosy.

"I should get back inside." He turned and opened the door.

"Hold on. What did you mean earlier, about warning him about Shelby?"

He stopped mid-step and turned around, his energy suddenly serious. "You don't remember? The way I see it, I chose the wrong girl that night."

I hadn't realized he regretted the way things turned out.

"I'm sorry, Tamara. Shelby is pretty, but she has no soul."

I threw him a confused look. "No soul?" Talk about harsh.

He hesitated, his hand still on the door. "I just don't want you to get hurt." He said quietly and then walked inside before I had a chance to respond.

What in the world was that supposed to mean, anyway? Yes, Shelby could be somewhat self-centered at times, but she was a good person. She'd never intentionally hurt me. In fact, there were several times she'd saved me when we worked together. Her taking the fall for me when my till was twenty dollars short ended up costing Shelby her job. But she seemed to do it gladly, and a week later, she found employment elsewhere. Shelby was a great friend. I was surprised she hadn't come to find me by now. Then again, she was probably busy putting the moves on the hot new stranger. My stomach turned at the thought, and something propelled me back inside.

Shelby, in full flirtation mode, was at the bar with Danny when I walked in.

"Hey, sweet stuff!" Shelby called out as I approached.

Danny turned, his stunning blue eyes landing on me.

Why hadn't I spent more time on my appearance before leaving the house? My hair was still damp, and I'd only put on a smidge of makeup.

"Danny, this is Tamara, my best friend and partner in crime."

He reached his hand toward mine, and I took hold of it. An electrical pulse jolted through me at his touch.

"Pleasure to meet you." He held my hand longer than expected. Was he feeling the same current I was?

"I was about to buy Danny a drink." Shelby propped her arm around his shoulder. I'd *never* seen her pay for a man's drink. A crazy urge to step between them shot through me. Ignoring the feeling, I took my place back at the bar, where my Coors Light still sat, getting warm.

Shelby flagged down Charlie.

"Hey, Danny, nice job on the mic." Charlie walked toward us, held up his hand, and gave him a high five.

"Thanks, man."

"What can I get you?"

"We'll take two Lemon Drops, and—" Shelby looked at Danny. "What are you having?"

"Hmm." Danny scanned the liquor shelf. "Lagavulin 16 sounds pretty good."

"And a Lagavulin for the charmer." Shelby looped her arm around Danny's.

"Coming right up." Charlie chuckled as if she'd made some sort of joke, turned around, and grabbed a bottle off the top shelf. He free-poured the whiskey into a small glass with a single cube of ice, then picked up a cocktail shaker and scooped ice into it. He threw in a few lemons and muddled it with the vodka, triple sec, and a touch of sugar. "That will be $22.50." He placed the drinks in front of us. Shelby's mouth dropped open.

Danny grinned and took a sip of his apparently very expensive drink.

Shelby opened her purse, pulled out twenty-five dollars, and slid it across the bar. "Keep the change."

My stomach clenched, and I reached for my wallet. I couldn't stick her with the tab like that. "I can get mine."

"I got it." She waved me off. "You can take care of the next round."

"Not if he's drinking." I chuckled nervously.

Danny laughed. "I'll pay for the next round. Thanks for the drink."

Shelby raised her glass in the air. "To a stunning performance by Danny McMillan."

We clicked our glasses together and shot them back. The vodka was smooth going down my throat and instantly warmed my insides.

Charlie took away my warm beer and replaced it with a fresh one. "You should never leave a drink unattended."

"Thanks." Hopefully, he wouldn't charge me for it.

"So, did you say you wrote that song? It was amazing." Shelby's slurring was getting worse by the moment. There had to be some way to slow down her drinking. Otherwise, I'd be babysitting her all night as she knelt before the porcelain throne.

"Yep," Danny responded. "Three days ago. It still needs some work, but I figured, what the heck?"

I was really digging his accent. "It was perfect. I wouldn't change a thing. I loved the prosody of it," I said.

He turned toward me, eyebrows raised. "Prosody?"

"The way the music and lyrics fit very well together."

"I know what prosody is. It's just a rare word, unless you're a musician. Do you play?" His gorgeous blue eyes were as deep as the ocean and as alluring as the song he'd sung. I felt as though I could fall into them.

"No, I just love music."

"What's your favorite type?" The corner of his mouth curled up into a sexy half-smile.

My fingers made a circle around the rim of my beer glass. "Well, I have a sweet spot for almost all Eighties music, but I love everything from Fleetwood Mac to Jamey Johnson."

"Jamey Johnson is a genius."

"Right?" I agreed and took a sip of my beer.

"What's your favorite song by him?"

"I'm thinking 'That Lonesome Song.'"

He studied me for a long moment, as if he was processing what I'd said. "Great answer."

"So, Danny." Shelby ran a finger down his arm in a provocative manner.

I ignored the desire to bat her hand away.

"Bob, the announcer, said you were from California. You

here visiting or what?"

"Something like that." He looked down at her hand like there was an unwanted insect on his arm. Was he actually impervious to Shelby's advances?

Charlie and I looked at each other, and he rolled his eyes.

"I've always wanted to go to Cali. I heard the beaches are way better there," Shelby said.

"Redding is a couple-hour drive from any beaches, so I didn't make it there as much as I would have liked. It's not like here, where it's just minutes away."

"Oh." Disappointment laced her tone.

"Hey, Shelby," Charlie said. "Where is Nick tonight?"

I choked on my beer. That was a great question. She and Nick had been getting pretty cozy lately. He wouldn't be happy if he saw the way Shelby was pawing at Danny.

Shelby glared at Charlie. "Don't you have other customers to tend to?"

Charlie looked around the room and then back at Shelby with a smug expression. "Everyone's taken care of for now."

"So, Tamara." Danny took a sip of his whiskey and turned back toward me. "I have a question for you." His gazed leveled on mine. "If you liked my song so much, why did you leave halfway through it?"

My heart fell into my stomach, and my cheeks instantly warmed. Not a question I was ready to answer.

"I was wondering the same thing." Shelby leaned over, eyes curious. "You missed the best part."

"I had a phone call." I looked up at Charlie, and he averted his eyes. "I'm sorry I missed it."

"I could sing it for you another time."

Heat spread through my stomach.

Did he just say he'd sing it for me? Like, *only* me? Be cool, Tamara. "I'd like that."

"Why don't we exchange numbers and hang sometime?"

Something dark flashed across Shelby's face. Was she mad that he had asked for my number instead of hers? Then she smiled and gave me an encouraging nod. Should I give him my number? Being around him made my heart do crazy, unpredictable things.

Somebody's gonna love you…

Was he supposed to be that somebody and I was too afraid to let that happen? Images of my nightmare engulfed my mind, filling me with dread. It was wrong of me to think about starting something with Danny when my demons were forcing me to leave town.

I looked up at Charlie. Why was he glaring a Danny?

My eyes met Danny's again. There was something about him that made it impossible to say no. Before I could think better of it, I asked Charlie to borrow his pen and ignored his reluctance as he handed it to me. I grabbed a napkin off the bar and scribbled down my number.

"Oh, no. Not good," Shelby slurred.

Her face had gone pale. "What's wrong?"

"The room just started spinning."

Of course it had. She probably hadn't eaten anything before her binge. In a quick moment, I was at her side, helping her off the stool.

"Do you want me to take you home?" I put my arm around her waist to steady her.

"That's probably a good idea." Her words were barely coherent.

I threw Danny an apologetic glance and then helped Shelby out to my car.

June 14, 11:13 p.m. – Danny

After Tamara left, I sat at the bar, staring at her number on the napkin. What was it about this girl? Dreams don't usually make themselves a reality, but the resemblance was strangely uncanny. Maybe after everything, my subconscious was messing with me. I picked up the napkin and then looked around the room. Behind the counter, Charlie seemed tense. Was he purposely avoiding eye contact with me? I'd noticed his glare when I asked for Tamara's number but hadn't understood it. Why would he care if I hung out with her?

At the end of the bar, there was an attractive brunette, sipping a martini. She caught my eye, smiled and raised her glass in my direction. I considered raising mine back, after all, a bit of distraction from the heartache I'd been through could be nice. I looked down at Tamara's number again. Another late-night bar hookup was *not* what I needed. That sort of behavior was what landed me here in the first place. I shot back the last of my whiskey, shoved Tamara's number into my pocket, and slid off the barstool.

The night air was cool on my way back to my uncle's bungalow. The smell of saltwater and seaweed calmed me as much as the sixteen-year-old scotch I'd just drank. Could Ocean Shores hold the healing my soul needed? I thought about

Tamara's lovely face and the girl from my dreams the other night. My subconscious seemed to think so. Perhaps God sent her my way to help put me back together?

What a ridiculous, romantic notion … but I'd always had a weakness for women. That's probably what made me a good songwriter. Too bad I was terrible at relationships … Perhaps I just hadn't found the right woman yet.

I looked up and took in a deep breath. The sky was clear, and the stars seemed closer than usual. "God, help me be a better man," I whispered.

Marisa and all that had happened between us flashed across my mind in a split-second, and my heart constricted in an excruciating way. Why couldn't I have been better then? Things could have been so much different. I swallowed back the lump that was forming in my throat and pulled out the napkin Tamara had written on. Asking for her number had probably been wrong. I was here to get away from the past. To heal from the wreckage. To die to my old life and be reborn. But somehow, I couldn't help myself. From the moment I saw Tamara in Midway's, something happened inside me that I couldn't explain. She was like a super-powered magnet, and I was simple metal with nothing to anchor me to the stage. Her soulful green eyes and the way she listened to me sing felt as if she had been pulling greatness out of me.

I took out my cell phone and programmed in her number. Then I deleted it. With my track record, I didn't deserve a girl like her. Should I have gotten Shelby's number instead? Having a fling with her and forgetting all the drama real love could bring was perhaps a better answer. But there was something about Tamara. She had depth. I could see in her eyes that she knew what it was like to feel pain like I had. Pressing the phone against my face, I closed my eyes and sucked in a sharp breath. My imagination immediately conjured up a picture of Tamara's face.

Her beautiful, angelic face.

Screw it.

I typed in her number again. Maybe I met Tamara tonight for a reason. Maybe she was part of the universe's divine plan. Maybe she could help me forget my past.

June 15, 9:42 a.m. – Tamara

I woke up with Danny's song on my mind—that, and his blue eyes, which were deep enough to lose my soul in.

Somebody's gonna love you …

Man, that sounded inviting. What would that even be like? The last person who'd claimed to love me made my life the empty void it was today. A life in which I always had to look over my shoulder to make sure I was safe.

Rolling over in bed, I grabbed my journal and pen and wrote to try to sort things out.

June 25
Something is seriously wrong with me. There was a guy at the bar last night, and I can't get him out of my head. Why is he affecting me like this? It doesn't matter! I just need to focus on saving money and getting the heck out of here. Love isn't something I can even dare to consider! Maybe one day … I'll have gone far enough, but for now, Ryan is only a couple of hundred miles away. It's stupid … no, it's lazy for me to stay in one place this long.

Throwing the journal and pen aside, I peeled myself out of bed. Writing wasn't helping, and I had to work today. Danny's lyrics kept playing through my brain as I took a shower and did my makeup. It was like a familiar, overplayed song on the radio, soothing yet frustrating in its redundancy. I needed to clear my head, so I threw on a hoodie, put my hair up and headed toward the ocean.

The weather was beautiful. Not quite ten o'clock and almost seventy degrees out.

Ten minutes later, I was standing in front of the ocean, the salty breeze blowing over my face. A beautiful distraction from the noise in my brain. Taking in a deep, cleansing breath, I reveled in the beauty of the waves, rolling and crashing against the shore. The vastness of the ocean always took my breath away. It made me think of how there had to be something out there bigger than myself.

God's gotta plan and a strong young man.

"*Do* You have a plan?" I said to the massive body of water. Pulling out a cigarette, I gazed out at the ocean. I struck the lighter, but the wind blew out the flame. After several more strikes, the flame caught, and I lit the smoke. My mind shifted to Ryan, my dad, and all the abuse in my past. There was no way God had a plan for me, and if he had, it was a twisted one.

God's gotta plan—

"Enough!" I screamed, a guttural response to the ridiculous song that wouldn't stop.

I reached down for something to throw into the ocean. A sand dollar poked out of the sand. I picked it up and a chill shivered down my spine. It was flawless. I sucked in another drag. I had searched this beach many times, looking for a perfect sand dollar, never to find one. To me, a complete sand dollar represented a whole life, unblemished and unshattered. I dusted the sand off its smooth ridges.

My phone dinged from my back pocket. I threw down my cigarette and pulled it out. The number that appeared on the screen was unfamiliar, so I opened the message.

`Hi, Tamara, it's Danny. How are you this beautiful morning?`

My heart rate doubled. Danny? I looked at the sand dollar in my hand. Too freaking bizarre.

`I'm good. How bout you?`

What a lame response. I didn't know the first thing about flirting via text. No matter. He most likely only wanted a friend in this new town. Otherwise, he would have asked Shelby for her number.

My phone dinged again.

`What are you up to?`

The words to his song filled my mind, and butterflies fluttered in my stomach. I looked out at the ocean and then back at my phone. What could I tell him? That I was unsuccessfully clearing my head from the spell he'd put me under last night? Not a chance.

`Getting ready for work.`

I typed the lie and hit send. When I gave him my number last night, I figured I wouldn't hear from him for at least a week, if at all.

`You like coffee?`

Love would have been a better word. Coffee was one of my favorite vices. Right up there with my smokes. They were terrible for me, but they'd been my faithful companions over the years. Always there when I needed them.

`I do.`

I shoved my phone in my back pocket and hightailed it to my house, the sand dollar still in my hand. I *did* need to finish getting ready for work.

The phone pinged again as I made it to my front door. I opened the door before pulling out my cell phone.

`You should meet me for a cup before work.`

I looked at my clock. 10:20 AM. That would be seriously pushing it.

`I don't have time.`

Pulling out my work uniform, I spread it across my bed. The outfit needed a thorough washing, but there was no time. Instead, I sprayed it with Febreze.

My phone dinged again.

`Just a quick cup. We could meet someplace close to your job.`

Biting my bottom lip, I stared at the screen. Giving him my number last night had been a huge mistake. Going out to coffee with him would probably be an even bigger one. I looked down at the sand dollar still in my hand and sighed. A cup of coffee wasn't going to hurt anything. For all I knew, he just needed a friend.

`Meet me at Beach Treasures in 20 mins.`

I finished doing my makeup in record time, threw my work clothes in a bag, and ran out the door.

June 15, 10:54 a.m. – Tamara

Driving would have saved time, but I thought better of it. Why waste the gas when it was such a beautiful day? Besides, it was only seven minutes from my house on foot. Five, if I speed-walked. That was another great thing about Ocean Shores, everything was in walking distance.

Danny was already sitting down at a table when I showed up, slouched in his chair with two cups of coffee in front of him. He was better-looking than I remembered. Or it could have been his five o'clock shadow. His scruffiness went well with the brooding musician motif. He wore cargo shorts and a Nirvana T-shirt.

"Sorry I'm late. You caught me off guard." I pulled up the chair and dropped my bag next to me.

"It's cool." He glanced at the sack, then looked up, his blue eyes catching my gaze. "Good to see you. You look pretty."

Heat tinged my cheeks. "Thanks." It had been way too long since I'd been on an actual date—if that's what this was. I wasn't sure how to respond. "You got me coffee?" I picked up the cup closest to me.

"Yes, I got a coffee how I think you like your men. Tall and strong."

"Oh, yeah?" I gave him a doubtful smile. "Why would you

think that?"

"You said yes to meeting me."

This *was* a date, then. "Nice one." I took a drink and made a face. It was way too strong. "I'm more of a sweet and creamy kind of girl."

He grinned. "I was kidding. That one is mine. I put cream and three sugars in this one." He passed me his cup to exchange it with mine.

I gladly scooted the bitter coffee over to him and made the switch. "Does that mean you like your women tall and strong?" I laughed, then took a sip. Way better. Good job, Danny.

"Beautiful and funny." His mouth quirked up into a smirk before taking a drink.

A small thrill ran through me at the fact that his lips were touching the cup where mine had just been.

"So, what's in the bag?"

Oh, man. Was he able to smell them? I so did *not* want to answer that question. "Work clothes. I didn't have a chance to wash them."

"Nice. I thought maybe you brought me something."

"Well, if you want my smelly work clothes, you can have them." I made a motion toward the bag.

"Thanks, but I'll pass." He scrunched up his face. "So, what do you do here in Ocean Shores?"

"For work or pleasure?" I fiddled with the edge of the coffee cup.

"Both."

"I work right over there." I nodded across the street. "Bennett's Fish Shack. And when I'm not working, on nice days, I'm down at the ocean, taking in the beauty. And then, of course, Midway's. But that's about all there is to do around here."

"So, no boyfriend?"

I shook my head. "I wouldn't be here with you if I had one."

"Excellent." He leaned back in his chair, his perfect lips curving into a broad smile. "The ocean part sounds amazing. And Midway's wasn't too bad. I met a really pretty girl there last night."

"Just one?" The women were surely flocking to him after Shelby and I left.

"Only one I was interested in." His eyes held mine, and it seemed as if they were sincere.

I lost myself in his gaze for a long moment, not sure how to respond to his words but feeling something deep and wild unfurl inside me.

"Tell me about yourself." Danny sipped his coffee.

"What do you want to know?"

"Are you from Ocean Shores?"

This is where things got tricky. How did I let someone in without telling them about my past? It had been easy with Shelby. She'd never tried to go deep. That's probably why we got along so well. "No, I've only been here for about ten months."

"Where are you from?"

"Here and there." It wasn't a lie. I'd been on the move for a few years. Well, more like on the run, but he didn't need to know about that.

"That's vague." He smiled, and a dimple popped in his left cheek. "And mysterious."

I averted my gaze. "Mysteries can be fun, right? What about you? What are you doing in Ocean Shores?"

"Following a dream." His voice was low and sounded far away.

Hadn't Charlie said something about him being here to get his head straight last night? And what about the stuff he'd said on the stage? Sounded like both of us were putting up a front.

Or both of us had things to hide. A part of me wanted to press him, but he hadn't pressed me. I should offer him the same respect. "In Ocean Shores? This doesn't seem like the right place for that."

"It's the artist's way. Sometimes, you need to go into hiding in order to come out on top. Kind of like a caterpillar turning into a butterfly."

I liked that analogy. Maybe I could frame my own life in that context. "What are you doing in this hiding place?"

"Writing my first album. My uncle is letting me stay in one of his beach houses for a while. I've been saving for the last few years, so I could take some time off and focus on writing and playing."

"That's really great." My crush was growing bigger every moment I spent with Danny. There was no doubt in my mind that someday the world would know this man. He not only had raw talent but a plan in place and the drive to follow through with it.

My phone buzzed, and I looked at it. A text from Shelby.

`My head hurts so bad. I'm never drinking again.`

I laughed. Shelby quit drinking? Yeah, right.

"What's funny?"

"It's Shelby. She's hungover." How would Shelby respond if she knew I was with Danny?

"Yeah … she seemed to be hitting it pretty hard last night."

I chuckled. "Just a little."

"Not you, though."

I shook my head. "I'm not a big drinker."

"I like that about you. You seem grounded." One side of his mouth tilted up. "Complete opposite of your friend."

"You didn't like Shelby?" That was surprising. Almost *every* guy liked her. At least, at first.

"She's all right. Just a bit too … how do I say this? Um. Shallow."

"I don't know whether to punch you or hug you." Yes, Shelby could be surface-level, but she was a good person. Yet, I couldn't help but feel a tiny bit of satisfaction that he seemed to like me and not her.

"I'll take option B." He grinned, and my heart skipped an irregular beat.

I looked at my phone again and noticed it was time to go. "I need to head to work." I grabbed my purse and work clothes and stood.

"Already?" He got up. "When can I see you again?"

"I work all weekend. Maybe Monday. Just call me."

"How 'bout that hug?"

I leaned in, and he put his arms around me. He smelled amazing, like citrus, lavender, and musk. My head swirled a bit at his touch. I looked up and stared into his gorgeous face. "I gotta go." I said but didn't move.

He tucked a lock of hair behind my ear, and his gaze landed on my lips. "See you soon."

My heart thrummed against my ribcage as his mouth edged toward mine.

My phone pinged again, breaking the spell.

I pulled away. "I'm going to be late." As I walked away, I could only think of one thing: I was in serious trouble. There was no way Danny and all his glory could fit into my world. But unless I left town today, I couldn't see myself being able to stay away from him.

June 15, 11:17 a.m. – Danny

As I sat finishing my coffee, I stared out at the ocean, thinking about my conversation with Tamara. What was her *real* story? Why was she so guarded about her past?

Eventually, I walked to Midway's for lunch. Charlie had told me to stop by, and he'd make me his famous Heart Attack burger. I wasn't really hungry. Being with Tamara had done a nice little number on my insides, and more than anything, I wanted to talk with someone who knew her.

I stepped inside the bar and looked around. Compared to last night, it was completely dead. There were a couple of guys at the bar with half-finished beers in front of them, probably drinking off last night's hangover.

"Hey, Danny," Charlie said as soon as he spotted me. "You ready for that Heart Attack?"

I slid onto a barstool. "Naw, man. I'll just have a Bud for now."

"Kinda early, isn't it?"

"It's five o'clock somewhere."

Charlie smirked as he grabbed a cold glass and filled it from the tap. "What's on your mind, cuz?"

"What's the deal with Tamara?"

He frowned and set the beer in front of me. "What about

her?"

"How well do you know her?"

Charlie cocked his head to the side. "Weren't you taking a break from women? I didn't think you came to Ocean Shores to date." His tone had a sharp edge.

What was with the attitude? "I'm taking a break from psycho-manipulative women. Tamara doesn't seem like that, so drop the crap." I picked up my beer.

Charlie slowly exhaled. "Tamara's a good person. She deserves better than a guy like you."

A guy like me? Kind of harsh. But there was something more in his words. "Do you have a thing for her?"

"Maybe." His gaze dropped to the floor. "But I dated her best friend. So, there's that." Charlie walked toward the two men at the other end of the bar and refilled their drinks.

I took a large swig of my beer.

Charlie grabbed a rag out of the bleach water and wrung it out before returning. "Here's the thing, Danny. What happened with your ex was seriously messed up, but we both know that you were no angel."

Damn. Charlie wasn't pulling any punches. "I hate myself for what happened with Marissa. But don't I deserve another shot?"

Charlie's eyes narrowed. "A shot? That's exactly what I'm talking about. It's not a game, man."

"Whatever. I shouldn't have brought it up."

"Why did you even come in here? For my approval? 'cause that's not going to happen." He scoffed.

"I don't need this." I stood. "I'm going for it."

Charlie leaned in, his expression hard. "How are you going to explain your arrest record?"

There it was. The truth was enough to knock me off-balance. If Tamara found out about my past, she'd never accept me. And if I hid it from her and she found out later, it would crush her. I sat back down.

"I'm never going to be free of it, am I?" I said, more to myself than Charlie. He was right. She did deserve better than a guy like me. I tilted back my beer and finished it in one shot.

June 28, 7:47 p.m. – Tamara

Nick added a piece of wood to the fire, and sparks flew upward. The sun was just about to set on this beautiful June day. It was my and Shelby's day off, and we decided to have a bonfire at the beach. The weather couldn't have been more perfect. Earlier, we'd swam for hours, and now, we were gathered around the fire. There were seven of us—Shelby and Nick, Savannah and Ethan, Milly and Caiden, and me. It wasn't unusual for me to be the lone ranger when hanging out with some couples, but ever since I'd had coffee with Danny, I had a hard time thinking about anything else.

I tried not to let it bug me, but it had been a while since I'd seen him, and I hadn't heard a word from him. I didn't understand. That day, he'd seemed genuinely interested, then… nothing. Complete silence for two weeks. I kept replaying that day because—whether I wanted to admit it or not—I really liked him. Had I misread his signals? It seemed like we had a connection, a spark that could easily ignite into a fire. It was probably better this way, though. Complicating my life with one more person was dangerous. I had been so hungry for what he seemed to be offering, I had lost sight of that fact.

"We should totally do it, right, Tam?"

I hadn't heard the rest of her comment. My eyes were on

the smoke as it drifted upwards, disappearing into the wind.

"Huh?" I looked up to see Shelby's questioning gaze.

"California road trip, baby."

I didn't want to think about California for the moment, or anything else that would remind me of Danny.

"We could go down Highway 101, like we always talked about, hitting every beach along the way."

"Sounds like fun." I tried to match her enthusiasm. I looked out at the water crashing against the shore and focused on the little foam bubbles each crest made. I didn't want other beaches.

And leaving Shelby would be unbearable. She was the reason I had stayed so long. I wished I could tell her everything and talk her into coming with me. It would be nice to have someone to travel with. Someone who really knew me. But I couldn't involve her in my drama. That would be selfish.

On the other hand, a road trip could solve my problem with Ryan. Everyone could chip in to get me far away from here, and then, I could stay down there. Anger welled in me at the thought, and I cursed Ryan for forcing me to leave this beautiful place, when all I wanted to do was stay.

"Well, well, well. Look, guys. It's the new town musician," Shelby said, her tone suddenly sour.

My head snapped up.

Danny was walking toward us with a bottle of beer in his hand.

My heart rate doubled.

"What are you doing here?" Shelby slung her arm around Nick's shoulder. "This is a private party." What was her problem with Danny? Had he ditched her too?

Danny made eye contact with me for a brief moment. Was that an apology in his eyes? I looked away.

"Just coming down to see who's making so much noise on my beach."

I could still feel his eyes on me. Did he want to talk to me? Why now?

"*Your* beach? What are you talking about?" Shelby stood and dusted herself off.

Danny lifted his beer toward the bungalow nearest to us. "That's where I live. You guys are in my front yard."

Seriously? Of all the places … I stood and turned to Shelby. "I'm going to head home."

"Okay—" Shelby said, confusion lining her features.

I turned away and walked up the path toward the road.

"Tamara, wait!" Danny called out.

I walked faster.

"Tamara, please." Twenty steps later, he took hold of my arm. "Can we talk?"

Swinging toward him, I looked into his eyes. "I'm pretty sure your silence said it all."

His grip tightened. "Let me explain."

My heart skipped several beats. "I'm listening."

His face was somber and full of longing. "I'm sorry I haven't texted or called. It's just—" He was quiet for a long moment. "Believe me, I wanted to. Every day."

"What do you want from me?" I tried to pull my arm from his grip, but he wouldn't let go.

He moved closer. "Someone whom I respect very much told me that I wasn't good enough for you." His voice was a whisper. "I had to admit that he was right." He paused and chuckled a little. "I can't believe I'm going to tell you this, but I watched you today."

My heart hammered against my chest and heat spread through me. Mesmerized by his face and the intensity in his voice, the words to respond to his confession didn't come. All I wanted was to hear more.

"You were there on the beach with your friends, swimming

and laughing, and everything in me knew that he was right. You *are* too good for me." A lock of dark hair fell over his face.

"Why are you telling me this?"

He looked down at his feet, seeming to struggle with the words he was about to say. "Because you make me want to be better."

We were both silent for a moment. In the background, there were sounds of the water washing up against the shore and the hushed whispers of my friends. Were they talking about us?

"I'm not as great as you think I am." If he only knew the mistakes I'd made, the people I'd hurt, he wouldn't be saying these words.

Danny nodded slowly. "It seems we both have a past."

"But that shouldn't define us, right?" I said.

He was quiet for a long moment, his expression pensive, like he was fighting an inner war. Finally, he spoke. "What do you say we start over? Come over tomorrow, and I'll make you dinner."

"I work 'til eight." He wasn't the only one fighting a battle. His closeness had turned my willpower to mush.

He gave a tentative half-smile. "So, it will be a late dinner, then."

I let out the breath I'd been holding. I'd probably regret it, but somehow, I couldn't say no. What was it about this guy? "Okay."

His eyes seemed happy and sad at the same time. "Eight-thirty, then?"

"Better make it nine." I'd want to shower and put on some makeup if this was a real date.

"Anything you hate or are allergic to?"

"Only games." How hypocritical was that? I was the one planning on leaving town without telling anyone.

"No games." He slowly released my arm. "I promise."

As he walked away, I looked back at my friends around the campfire. Shelby stood with her arms crossed, and eyes narrowed. My heart thudded three times before she dropped her arms and stalked off.

June 29, 10:45 a.m. – Tamara

The next morning, Shelby called as I was getting ready for work. I'd been dreading talking to her, since she'd stormed off last night. The thought of her accusing glare haunted me for hours, and then I fell asleep and had the nightmare again, but this time, someone else was there, holding me down as Ryan choked me.

Here it goes.

Ignoring the images, I took in a deep breath and answered the phone. "Hello."

"What was that last night? What is going on with you and Danny?"

"Good morning to you too, Shelby." I tried to joke away my anxiety.

"Last I checked, we were best friends. You hooked up with Danny and didn't even tell me?"

I rolled my eyes. So dramatic. She actually thought I slept with him? "Calm down now. Nobody hooked up with anyone."

"That's not what it looked like last night."

She had me there. It did look suspicious, but it wasn't like anything actually happened. I wasn't even sure what to think of him showing up yesterday. Or going to his house tonight. It felt … dangerous … and exhilarating. "He asked me out for coffee the day after we met."

"And?" Shelby huffed.

"That was it. He never called or texted after that. I thought maybe he left town."

"Then why the dramatics?" She demanded. "Why did you leave when he showed up if nothing happened?"

Closing my eyes, I pinched the bridge of my nose. This conversation was exhausting. "It just threw me off. I don't know how to explain it. When we had coffee together, it seemed like there was a connection, and then he didn't call or text. It felt like he was messing with my head. But he apologized last night."

A brutally long silence drug out. Had she hung up? I looked at the screen, but the call was still connected. If she was reacting this strongly over us having coffee, I couldn't possibly bring myself to tell her I was planning on seeing him tonight.

"You still there?"

"Yeah, I'm just worried about you. Something seems off with the whole thing. I don't want you seeing him again. I mean, what do you even know about this guy?"

She couldn't be serious. Who did she think she was? The one time a guy chooses me over her, she pulls out the caution card? Sure, I didn't know much about him but neither did she when she was hanging all over him that night at the bar. Danny didn't seem like a bad guy. And wasn't the purpose of dating getting to know each other? "I'll find out more about him tonight."

"What? You're seeing him again? Tonight? *Tamara.*"

"No, Shelby, don't *Tamara* me. You are just jealous he chose me over you."

More silence. My stomach swam with anxiety. How would Shelby react to that rebuke?

After the long pause came a deep exhale. "I'm sorry you feel like that. I'm just worried about you."

My heart softened. I didn't want to fight with Shelby.

Especially not over a guy I barely knew. "I appreciate your concern, but I'll be okay. He seems like a nice guy."

"I just don't want you getting hurt. I'd have to kill someone, and there are not enough places around here to hide the body."

I let out a nervous laugh. At least she was making light of the situation. "I'm sure I'll be fine."

"We'll see about that. Tell Danny I have my eye on him." What was that in her voice—amusement, or a threat?

I held out the phone and gave it a perplexed look. I'd never seen Shelby act so protective of me before. Then again, she'd never seen me interested in someone. I noticed the time at the top of the screen. "I need to get ready for work."

"Okay, but you better give me details about tonight. If Danny steps out of line at all—"

I let out an exasperated sigh. "Oh, my goodness. I'll be fine. Danny is a decent guy."

"We'll see about that." Her words sounded ominous. As if she knew something I didn't.

My stomach tightened. Had Charlie told her something he refused to share with me? Whatever it was, I was beyond done with this conversation. "I really gotta go. Love you."

I hung up before she could put any more doubts in my head about tonight.

June 29, 7:56 p.m. – Tamara

Work ended up being super slow, so my boss let me go an hour early. When I got home, I stripped off my smelly, fish shack clothes, cleaned up, and dressed nicely. I wore a pair of Miss Me jeans Shelby had given me for my birthday, a flowy, light-pink top, and brown boots. I checked out myself in the full-length mirror, and my stomach did a large flip-flop. What in the world was I doing? Going over to Danny's tonight was a mistake. Nothing good could come of it.

Somebody's gonna love you …

Shaking my head, I looked around for my journal and finally found it wedged between the bed and the nightstand. I sat on the bed and wrote.

Why am I flirting with disaster? Why am I allowing myself to go deeper down this rabbit hole? Danny's song keeps playing in my head. He's like the pied piper, and I'm under some strange enchantment. My heart keeps telling me that his song was written just for me, but there is no way that's possible. I feel like some foolish little girl, hoping for someone to rescue me from this lonely existence. Going over there tonight is only setting myself up for heartbreak. Maybe I should stand him up and save us both the trouble.

Sighing deeply, I sunk deeper into my bed, loneliness weighing down my body. A tear slid down my cheek. Couldn't I just pretend for one night I was a normal twenty-year-old girl and let myself get caught up in something that could be … amazing … thrilling … exhilarating? I searched my heart for a second and tried to push away all the fears, doubts, and what-ifs. Honestly, I wanted to go tonight, even if it ended up hurting me. The thought of not going almost hurt worse.

I rose and went back into the bathroom to finish getting ready. After applying a large amount of product to my hair, I blew it out and teased it, giving it extra body. I ran eyeliner along my lids and brushed on mascara. I finished off my makeup by highlighting my high cheekbones with blush and then dabbing on a bit of lip gloss. It was more effort than I'd put into my appearance in a long time. Shelby would be proud. Well, she would if she actually approved of my date, but that was something else I couldn't think about now.

I threw on a light jacket and headed out the door, securing the lock on the way out. The air outside was a bit damp, but I didn't mind. I loved to breathe in the fresh ocean air as I walked. When I approached Danny's house, there was a pizza delivery car pulling away. Wasn't he supposed to be making dinner?

I rang his doorbell.

Seconds later, he opened the door, wearing faded blue jeans and a snug white T-shirt that sported the lean muscles of his chest and biceps. "Welcome." He grinned and his dark hair fell over his face. "You look lovely." Stepping aside, he made a sweeping gesture with his hand. "I was just finishing up the salad." A cozy warmth hit me as I stepped through the door, along with the slight smell of something burnt hovering in the air.

The house was small and open. The front door led into the

living room. It had a cherry-wood floor with a red-and-black area rug in the center. Circling the rug was a tan futon, two gray chairs, a table, and a small TV. An acoustic guitar leaned against the wall. On the table was a notepad and pen. Danny's songbook, possibly? A bar separated the living room from the kitchen. On the bar, there was a checkered pizza box and a bowl of salad.

"Pizza?" I lifted a questioning brow.

He gave me a crooked smile. "Well, I was making you love dumplings, but unfortunately, I burnt the crap out of them."

"Love dumplings? Really?" I laughed.

He shrugged, his smile growing wider. "Found them on Pinterest."

I laughed harder. "Pinterest? Really?" He was too adorable.

"You don't Pinterest things?"

"It's called 'pinning.'" I shook my head, still laughing. "And no, I detest all social media." I hated anything that would make it easier for Ryan to track me. For the most part, I stayed off the Internet.

He raised his hands in the air. "Okay, I admit, I'm not a fan of 'pinning' either." He said, using air quotes. "It's just that I haven't dated for a while, so I searched for romantic dinner ideas and Pinterest was the first thing that came up."

"Oh. You want this to be romantic?" Unease swirled in my stomach. Was he being sincere or just playing me?

"Absolutely, don't you? This is a date, right?" He sounded concerned.

"Sure, I think so. I actually don't really date much either, but I am pretty sure in order for it to be romantic, there needs to be less burnt food and delivered pizza." I gave him a pointed look and tried not to laugh.

"Oh… burn." He followed me into the kitchen.

"Exactly, that's what I'm saying." I spun around to face him and grinned. The joking around put my nerves at ease, but something in me hummed at his closeness.

"You're enjoying my screw-up a bit too much, don't you think?" Danny took a step closer to me. "At least I *tried* to make you dinner."

"True." His burnt attempt was much more than I'd received from any guy in a long time. The pizza did smell good if I ignored the lingering scent of the scorched "love dumplings" in the background.

"And I do want to kiss you." His voice was barely more than a whisper.

My face heated and my pulse sped up. "Oh yeah?"

He came in closer, his lips an inch away from mine. "Yeah." His hand touched my neck and then drifted up to cradle my jaw.

I stopped breathing.

His mouth touched mine, softly and sweetly.

I felt the kiss everywhere from my head to my feet, inside and out.

He leaned back and moaned so quietly, I could barely hear it. "Sorry, I had to get that out. I've been thinking about doing that for almost two weeks."

And I'd be thinking about it for the next two weeks. It had been a long time since I'd been kissed, but I didn't remember it feeling anything like that. I pushed away before I could pull myself back into him. "Oh, wow, okay, well, um, how about that super-romantic pizza now?"

"Not just pizza." He chuckled as he sauntered to the fridge and pulled out a bottle of champagne. "This was supposed to go well with the love biscuits."

"This date just got ten times classier," I teased.

Unwrapping the bottle, he worked at uncorking it. "'Classy' is my middle name." He twisted his hand and the cork popped off. Foam oozed down one side. He snagged a few wine glasses from the cupboard, poured us each a glass and handed me one. His eyes landed on my mouth. Was he thinking about the kiss? Because I sure was. I wanted to kiss him again, but I took a sip of the champagne instead.

His eyes stayed on me like he was fascinated. "Speaking of middle names, what is yours?"

"A bit too personal of a question for a first date, don't you think?" I winked.

"I'll tell you mine if you tell me yours." A sexy smile crept onto his face.

He was too darn irresistible. "Christine."

"No way. Mine too." He took a sip from his cup, lips twitching as they held back a smile.

I smacked him playfully on the arm. "It is not."

He grabbed my hand and pulled me in close, wrapping his arms around my waist. "I already told you my middle name. It's Classy."

"You're such a liar." I glowered at him.

"Are you implying that I'm not classy?" His perfect lips were so tempting.

"Maybe." I giggled.

His mouth met mine again, deeper and more sensual. He leaned back after a moment, a smile tugging at his lips. "Scott."

"Huh?" My head spun from the kiss. I'd forgotten what we were talking about.

He laughed. "My middle name." He released me. "You hungry?"

There were all sorts of stuff happening in my stomach, but hunger didn't seem to be one of them.

He grabbed the pizza box and his glass of champagne. "Come on, let's move to the couch."

I followed him to the living room and sat down next him.

"Tell me more about you," he said, setting the pizza and a

couple of paper plates on the small coffee table.

I sipped on the glass of champagne. "What do you want to know?"

"Favorite band?" He opened the box of pizza. It looked like half-supreme, half-Hawaiian. He picked up a piece piled with meat and took a bite.

"Oh, man, that's really tough. Right now, probably Passenger." I grabbed a piece of supreme pizza as well, picked a slice of pepperoni off it, and popped it in my mouth.

"You like Passenger?" He said mid-chew, sheltering his mouth with his hand.

I finished chewing my bite and gulped it down. "*Love.*"

"Okay, what's your favorite song by them?" He set his pizza down and turned toward me.

I took another drink of my bubbly. "Hmm. Probably 'Feather on the Clyde.'"

"Oh, man. See, this is why I'm falling in like with you." He scooted closer to me and put his hand behind me, brushing it against my back.

I set my pizza down and leaned into him. "Falling in like?" My eyes met his. His gaze was more intoxicating than the wine.

He caressed my back, working his fingers up to my neck.

My skin tingled every place he touched.

"Well, it's too soon to say 'love,' right?"

"Probably." Was this the beginning of love? It was so weird to think about such things. We seriously just met, but from the moment I met him—no, from the moment I saw him on that stage, the moment I heard him sing, I was a goner.

"So, that's the next-closest thing." He moved in closer and kissed me again.

I loved the way his lips felt as they softly met mine. I could feel myself becoming addicted to them.

"That's the thing, Tamara. I really like you."

Opening my eyes, I stared into his electric blues, and my heart thudded loudly. I reached for my drink to take another sip, but it was empty.

"I love the fact that your favorite Passenger song is 'Feather on the Clyde,'" he said. "You ask most people, they'd probably say, 'Let Her Go,' and don't get me wrong, it's a great song. But they probably heard it on the radio. But you, you heard the greatness that I heard in that song and went and bought the album and maybe even realized that Passenger was a musical genius."

I nodded. He'd pretty much nailed it.

"Sorry, I get a bit passionate about this stuff."

"It's great. Music has always been my first love."

"It's my religion." He downed the last of his drink. "Would you like some more champagne?"

"Actually, I think a beer would be a lot better with this pizza."

He laughed. "Prefers beer to champagne. One more thing to love about you." He stood and walked to the kitchen.

I rose and followed him. "'Love' is a really strong word." Caution formed a pit in my stomach. This was the second time he had said the 'L' word in the last five minutes. That was a bit much for a first date.

Danny pulled me in close again. "Strong, but fitting." He kissed me again, but this time, it was fierce and passionate.

My body responded in a wild, unexpected way, and desire ignited inside me. For a moment, I let myself get lost in the passion before reason set in. Was this why he'd brought me here? To seduce me? He knew how to say all the right things, and I had almost bought into it. What an idiot I was. I stiffened and pulled away.

"What's wrong?" he said, breathless.

I struggled for words as I caught my breath. I kept my gaze

on the floor as I spoke. "Listen, I don't know what this is, but if you're looking for a one-night stand, you got the wrong girl's phone number."

Silence dragged on for a few merciless seconds. Then I felt Danny come closer. His finger gently came under my jaw, and he pulled my face toward his. "I'm not looking for a one-night stand, Tamara. I swear to you, I did everything I could to get you out of my mind over the last couple of weeks, but when I saw you yesterday, I knew I couldn't run from it anymore."

My head spun, intoxicated by his words. A part of me wanted to run out the door, while the other part wanted to finish what we started. I searched his eyes and drew in a deep breath. "The thing is, Danny, I've been alone for a long time. I'm not afraid of it. But somehow, you've awakened something in me. What I'm terrified of is letting you in and then getting my heart broken." The words came out shaky and hoarse. "I'm pretty sure I've had enough heartbreak to last a lifetime."

"Oh, beautiful girl—believe me when I say this—I'll do everything in my power to never hurt you." He wiped away a tear that I hadn't realized had fallen down my cheek.

"Maybe we should take things a bit slower then," I whispered. "For my heart's sake."

"Absolutely." His smile was sad as he ran his fingers through my hair. "Let's go sit down and have some more pizza and talk." He slowly pulled away, grabbed our beers off the counter and took his place on the futon.

I blinked a few times, unsure of what had just happened. It had been years since I'd been that vulnerable with someone. Being around Danny was doing strange things to me. The urge to bolt out the door hit me once more.

"You coming?" He patted the spot next to him. "I promise to be good."

"You'd better be." I laughed, slipping back into our playful banter. I took a seat next to him on the couch and hoped for the best. It occurred to me then that I had come here tonight for the same reason he'd come to me on the beach yesterday. It was almost impossible to fight the magnetic connection that was drawing us to each other.

July 2, 5:56 p.m. – Danny

I scanned the jukebox at Midway's as I waited for Tamara, thinking about our last few days together. That first night, we'd stayed up until three in the morning, talking, laughing and kissing. She'd eventually fallen asleep in the crook of my arm. For the longest time, I just watched her, my heart doing crazy things. As I held her, I felt like I was holding an angel. Perhaps that's what she was. Being around her helped me forget the past. I wished so badly we could stay in this place, and I could forget my old life forever, but the moment would come when I had to tell her, and it needed to come soon.

"Hey." Tamara's voice came from beside me.

I turned toward her.

She looked the same way she had the first night I met her, hair still damp. Her eyelashes were tinged with mascara, accenting her vibrant green eyes, and her cheeks were still flushed from the shower. Beautiful.

I put my arms around her and kissed the top of her forehead. She smelled like ocean mist and vanilla. "How was work?" I pulled back to see her face.

"Considering my lack of sleep—" We exchanged a knowing smile. "It wasn't too bad. Just was really anxious to get out of there."

"I got us a pitcher of beer."

"This is why I'll keep you around." She kissed me a small peck on the mouth, and then pulled away to pour herself a glass.

From the corner of my eye, I noticed Charlie tense and avert his gaze. Fresh guilt hit my stomach as our conversation played in my head. What was I thinking, coming here with Tamara tonight? When I was alone with her, it was easy to pretend I wasn't the guy I used to be.

"Is it weird to say I missed you today?" Tamara's voice pulled me out of my self-loathing.

I put my hand on the small of her back. "Is it weird to say I missed you back?"

Smiling, she slid her arms around my neck. "Naw." She kissed me and for a brief moment, I was able to forget again.

Tamara's phone buzzed. She pulled away from me and took it out of her back pocket. For a few seconds, she seemed unsure about answering it before finally hitting the talk icon.

"Hey, chica, what's up?" She listened for a beat and said, "No. I'm at Midway's with Danny." There were a few more beats of silence as she listened. "Uh, okay, yeah. We'll be here for a little while." She ended the call but stared at the phone with an uneasy expression on her face.

"Everything okay?" I caressed her shoulders.

"I'm not sure." She seemed apprehensive. "Shelby said she needed to talk to me. She said it was urgent."

"That doesn't sound good." Trepidation crawled along my spine. I pounded the rest of my beer and poured another glass. Tamara chewed her bottom lip and messed with her phone.

A few minutes later, Shelby rushed through the door and spotted us. She stalked toward us, a piece of paper in her hand. "You're gonna want to see this." She glared at me and then handed the paper to Tamara. "It's amazing what you can find on the Internet." She shot me another dirty look.

My stomach felt like the Hiroshima bomb had exploded inside it. What had she found? Why would she even look?

"What is this?" Tamara glanced at me and then back to the paper.

"No clue." I tried to read it over Tamara's shoulder, but she backed away, hiding the paper. Her eyes widened as she scanned the page. She took her time, seeming to read it carefully.

Self-hatred tightened its grip around my soul. Why hadn't I told her myself? Things had been going so well. The timing hadn't seemed right, but it wasn't supposed to go like this. Sometimes, I hated life. Right when I thought things were turning around—*bam,* sucker punch. All the air was knocked from my lungs.

When she looked back up at me, her face was full of shock and revulsion. Then she bolted out the door.

July 2, 6:15 p.m. – Tamara

Dark clouds gathered overhead as I ran toward the ocean. This couldn't be happening. Oh, wait a second, of course it could. This was my life. My disgusting, mixed-up life. The first guy I happened to let my guard down with would have that kind of record. Why was I always drawn to abusers?

I ran harder. I just needed to think. But what good would thinking do?

Perhaps this was the push I needed to finally leave town. My money jar was still pretty empty, but I didn't care. I would make do.

The water came into view, and I slowed to catch my breath. The wind blew hard around me as the waves began to swell. A part of me wanted to wade in deep and get lost in the undertow. Instead, I stepped out onto the dock.

Despair choked my heart. Danny had seemed like a glimmer of hope. He had awoken a hunger in me I hadn't known I'd been suppressing since Ryan. His arms were an empty promise, a golden carrot dangled in front of me, only to be snatched away. Rain pelted my face and another gust of wind whipped around me. The dock swayed beneath my feet. For a long time, I just stood on the edge, imagining myself jumping into the turbulent waters, letting the waves drowned the sorrow of this lonely life. I fell to my knees on the rough wood and cried.

I leaned over the edge vaguely making out my silhouette between the raindrops. Looking down at the water, my distorted face stared back at me, taunting me, reminding me I would never be free of my choices. Why did I keep doing this? What was I thinking, letting myself fall for someone like Danny? First, Ryan now, Danny. I keep attracting the same kind of guy. They were all lying, pond-scum jerks.

The paper Shelby gave me thundered through my mind. *Domestic violence.* The words stabbed me in the guts. Convicted in a court of law of aggravated assault on his pregnant ex-girlfriend. It was so much worse than dealing drugs. Danny, the man who could play such a sweet song one day, could go home and lay hands on a pregnant woman the next? The heat left my body, leaving me frigid, betrayed, shocked, and furious.

I screamed and swore at my reflection.

Danny was suddenly next to me. "Tamara, please. I promise you what you read isn't true."

"Get away from me." The words seethed out of my mouth. I wished I could believe him. My traitorous body wanted his arms around me. Innocent until proven guilty, right? Well, those papers said "guilty." Sentenced to three months in jail.

"Please, just let me tell you. Every awful detail of the story is false. I would never hit a woman, Tamara. You have to believe me." He caressed my arm.

My heart responded to his touch. How could these gentle hands be ones that abused a woman?

"Marisa and I had been together since I was seventeen. We met when we lived in Philly, but shortly after she graduated from high school, her dad got a job in Redding."

It was raining big drops now, and the wind howled around us. I started to shiver.

"You're freezing. Could we finish this conversation back at

my place, where it's warm?"

I shook my head, pulled back from his embrace, and got to my feet. I wasn't going anywhere with him.

"Tamara, please listen!" He yelled at me over the heavy rain.

I turned around. His deep, tortured eyes pleaded for me to believe him. "What happened?" Could I even handle the answer?

"Things got hard for us after a few years in Redding." Rain ran down his face. "I wanted to pursue my music career, but I was bogged down at a job I hated. Marisa was happy in Redding. She wanted to settle down there and start a family. She told me all the time that my dreams were unrealistic." Danny's gaze darkened a bit as he told the story. "That I was selfish to continue to go after them. One night, we got in a huge fight, and I went drinking with my friends. We were partying hard. I was drunk and very angry. This pretty young woman kept throwing herself at me all night. In my mind, Marisa and I were over anyway. We were only making each other miserable by staying together."

Chills racked my body. I knew where this was headed. Danny had cheated. Even if he hadn't hit her, did I want to involve myself with a guy who would cheat?

"The next morning, I went home to tell her the truth. We were over. That's when she dropped the bomb. She was pregnant. I told her I'd absolutely be there for her and the baby, but I couldn't keep living my life in that sort of misery. Marisa went ballistic. She began hitting me and then hitting herself, like, really hard in the face. I tried to restrain her and get her to calm down, but she started biting and scratching me. I finally called the cops, but when they got there, she told them I did it to her, and they believed her fabricated story over mine."

I searched Danny's face. All I could see was sincerity and truth. I knew what it was like to be touched by an abuser. There was nothing in me that felt his hands would ever harm me.

"Please, Tamara, say something. Tell me you believe me.

I didn't know if it was because I was already in completely over my head with him but my heart told me he was telling the truth. "I do."

Relief washed over his beautiful face. "Can we please get you out of the cold?"

Teeth chattering, I nodded.

He put his arm around me. "Let's go get you warmed up before you get sick."

July 2, 6:46 p.m. – Tamara

When we got back to Danny's house, he turned up the heat and pulled off his wet shirt. "You need to take a hot shower."

Shivering, I stared at the lean muscles of his chest and shoulders and swallowed. "I don't have any clothes."

He walked into his room and returned a moment later, holding sweatpants, a T-shirt, and a hoodie. "Take as long as you need to warm up."

"What about you?"

His eyebrows shot up. "Do you want me to join you?"

Blood rushed to my face. "No—" I shook my head. "Um, I meant, aren't you cold?"

A grin broke over his stunning features. "I'll be just fine. I'm not the one whose lips were turning blue out there."

"Okay." I turned and walked to the bathroom. It took me a minute to figure out how to work his shower. The hot turned on when I turned it clockwise, instead of counterclockwise, like in my apartment.

As the hot water ran over my skin, I thought about Danny's story. How awful that must have been for him to spend three months in the county jail for something he would never do. He *had* cheated, though. That was a huge strike against him, but from the sound of it, they were practically broken up anyway.

And it *was* possible for people to change. I had made my fair share of mistakes in the past. Who was I to throw stones at Danny?

I shut off the water and grabbed the towel. The sound of Danny strumming his guitar and singing the song he'd played at Midway's the other night came through the door.

"Somebody's gonna love you,
carry you back home.
To hell with the rain. It's a magical day."

I loved the resonance of his voice. It struck my heart like a musician playing the strings of a violin.

"It's a done deal. It's written down in stone.
So, go, baby, go, baby, go, baby, go.
Don't close your eyes. You're a heartbeat away, just south of paradise."

I pulled on his sweats and threw on his T-shirt and hoodie. The hoodie smelled like that citrusy-lavender cologne he wore. His clothes were at least three sizes too big for me, but I was thankful to be warm.

Pushing the bathroom door open, I expected to see Danny, sitting on the couch with his guitar, but he wasn't there. I followed the music into his bedroom, where he sat, still shirtless, on the bed. Heat pulsed through my veins.

Danny looked up. He sucked in a sharp breath and his countenance seemed somewhat awestruck.

"What is it?"

He set his guitar aside and motioned for me to come to him. When I was close, he pulled me onto his lap. A slow thrill ran through me. I was in *his* bedroom with him on *his* bed. I knew where this was going and didn't think I could stop it, even if I wanted to. There were still so many questions I had about his past. There were still so many things I hadn't told him about mine. Would getting physical this soon blur any lines of reasoning I had? I placed my head on his bare chest.

One of his hands rested on my thigh, the other on the small of my back. I could hear the thrumming of his heartbeat.

"Tell me your thoughts," he said.

I breathed in deeply, enjoying being in his arms. "I have a lot of questions."

"I'll tell you anything you want to know." His hand traced circles on my legs.

My skin warmed where he touched, but it sent chills through the rest of my body. It was super distracting. "You said your ex was pregnant?"

Danny became still. "She's six months pregnant. I'm not sure of the exact due date." He paused, seeming to struggle with his words. "That's what kills me the most. I don't know if I'll ever be allowed in my child's life."

I brought my hand to his bare chest, pressing into his firm muscles and soft skin. "I'm sorry."

"It's awful, but I'm doing my best to let the past go. And to be responsible. I've already put some money aside for the baby. It's in a CD, so I won't be able to touch it. I'll do more over the years, and when they're old enough, it will be a college fund or whatever."

"That's really great. Your child is lucky to have a dad who cares like that." I thought of my dad and how big the contrast was. "Even if you can't be a part of their life right now." I lifted my head off his chest. Our gazes met.

A fire burned behind his eyes, a mixture of desire and amazement. "It means everything to me that you believe me and accept me." His lips touched my cheek and made their way to my ear. "You're my angel."

Tingles ran down my spine and through my body.

"Remember at the bar, when I talked about the girl in my dream that saved me from myself?" He threaded his fingers through my hair and pulled me in closer. "It's you, Tamara. I knew it from the moment I saw you that night, and I saw it again when you walked into my room just now." His lips caressed my neck. "What about you, Tamara? What are you running from?"

His words pulled me out of the moment and suddenly, I wanted to cry. I didn't want to think about my past, let alone talk about it. "What do you mean?"

"Come on, now, don't deny it. I can see it in your eyes. The way you deflect questions about where you're from."

Swallowing the knot that was forming in my throat, I closed my eyes, trying to push away the memories of the day I'd left home, beaten and bloody. "Let's just say I know what it's like to have hands laid on me." I opened my eyes.

Compassion lined Danny's features. "No wonder you freaked out when you read that paper. You must have thought I was a complete monster." He brought his hand to my face. "But I'd never hurt you. Not like that."

I believed him, but there was so much more of my story to tell. Was I ready to open up to him about all my junk? These secrets had been buried deep down for so long, it felt like if I spoke them out loud, they'd consume and overtake me.

"It's okay. You don't have to talk about it." He whispered. "There's just one thing I'd like to know. Who's Ryan?"

My heart jolted and my body went rigid. "Where did you get that name?"

"You said it when you were asleep the other night." Lines appeared in his forehead.

He had trusted me with his demons, why couldn't I trust him with mine? I took another long breath. "Ryan is my ex-boyfriend. I didn't know he was a meth dealer when we got together." I paused for a moment, editing the story in my head. "It was dumb. I know. I lived with him for about a month without even realizing it. You know what they say, love is blind." More like youth and stupidity.

"The night I found out, I stole a couple grand from his wallet and skipped town and never looked back. For a couple years, I didn't stay in one place long, always afraid he'd be looking for me." There was so much more to the story, but I wasn't ready to talk about that now.

He gave me a skeptical look. "You think he'd still be looking for you over a couple grand?"

It was a legitimate question. But he didn't know what Ryan was capable of. Memories of Ryan kicking the crap out of that kid over two hundred dollars caused the room to seem darker. *"You screwed me over, boy! I'll make you bleed and watch you die."* The distant memories of Ryan's voice made my head ache.

"I don't think he'll ever give up. I was gearing up to leave town right before we met."

Danny's slid his arms around my waist, drawing me in closer. "You don't have to worry about that anymore. I won't let anyone hurt you."

I nuzzled into his chest. I did feel safe with him. He said I was saving him, but maybe he was saving me. He pulled my hair back and kissed my neck up toward my ear. "I'm falling for you, Tamara," he whispered.

"I'm falling for you, too."

His lips found mine again, and in that moment, I was completely lost to him.

July 3, 8:34 a.m. – Danny

When I woke, Tamara was curled around me. I wanted so badly to wake her up just to make love again, but she was so beautiful and peaceful, I couldn't do it. Instead, I watched her sleep and thought about how lucky I was that I'd met her when I did. Everything Marisa had done to me had left me a broken mess of a man. But being with Tamara made that all go away. She couldn't change the past, but perhaps she'd be my future.

A prickle of doubt nudged me. Would I ever be worthy of Tamara? After everything that I'd done, it was selfish of me to pursue her. She *did* make me want to be a better man, though. Hopefully, love would be enough to slay the beast inside, because one thing I was absolutely sure of was that I was falling in love with this woman.

She stirred a tiny bit.

Dark hair fell across her porcelain skin. Man, she was lovely. Angelic. In my heart, that's what she was. I caressed her cheek, and lyrics flitted through my mind.

What's left of that girl is a fallen angel.

Careful not to disturb her, I slid my arm out from under Tamara's head. She stirred again, but only for a moment. I quietly climbed out of bed, slid on some sweats and a T-shirt, and grabbed my guitar. On the way out to the front deck, I picked up my songbook. Mornings were the best time to write music. A few weeks ago, the song I wrote had been inspired by a dream. Today, that dream was lying in my bed, and more inspiration was coming.

I'll gladly take what's left of that girl.

The morning was beautiful. Last night's storm had passed and brought this peaceful calm. Before me was the vast ocean, full of power and splendor, but if I turned around, I could see a large, majestic mountain range. Breathtaking. A warm melody came into my heart, and more lyrics along with it. I sat down with my guitar and played around with a few chords to go along with the melody in my mind. More lines to the song came.

I was born in an American town
where the mountains touched the face of God,
and she was born on the wrong side of the tracks.

I thought about Tamara lying in my bed. There were still so many things I didn't know about her. I didn't even know where she'd grown up. The only thing I knew was that she'd been on the run for a while.

A city girl with a life full of pain,
picked her up in the pouring rain,
thumbing her way to nowhere from the past.

Placing my guitar on the seat next to me, I gazed at the ocean. Small waves rolled up over the shore, while seagulls roamed around, searching for their breakfast. How could this woman I barely knew inspire such music in me?

"I could get used to this, you know." Tamara's voice startled me. She stood on the patio, wrapped in a blanket, hair disarrayed from sleep.

"Used to what?" I stood, and the lawn chair creaked a bit.

"Being serenaded first thing in the morning." A lazy smile hung on her lips.

I came to her and wrapped my arms around her. "I'll serenade you anytime you want."

"You shouldn't make promises like that. I might become greedy."

I chuckled and pressed my lips against her forehead. "You hungry? I could make you breakfast."

She looked up at me, eyes dancing. "You sure you won't burn it?"

"I think I can handle it." I poked her in the sides, and she giggled.

"I guess I could give you another chance, and I will be there to supervise this time."

Shaking my head, I grinned. "You're never going to let me live that down, are you?"

"Nope." Her smile was playful, alluring.

I placed my hands on her hips and kissed her. "Or we could go back to bed."

She moaned. "I wish, but I have to leave soon to get ready for work."

"Can't you call in sick?" My lips caressed her neck.

"Don't tempt me."

I nibbled on her ear. "But I *like* tempting you."

She moaned again. "You're definitely good at it, but I do need to work."

I pulled back, so I could see her face. "You're so good,

Tamara. You shouldn't let a guy like me corrupt you."

"I'll try not to. Now, how about that breakfast?"

I kissed the tip of her nose. "All right, fine. No bed, just breakfast."

She laughed. "Sounds like *you're* the greedy one."

"There's no denying that." I took her by the hand and led her back inside.

July 3, 9:37 a.m. – Tamara

As I walked back to my apartment, I pulled out my phone. There were six missed calls and eleven new text messages—all from Shelby. My heart rate increased. Last night, she had only meant to protect me. Not only did I ignore her concern, I ran in the other direction, slept with Danny, and ignored her in the process. I was a horrible friend. I read the messages.

`Tamara, you need to call me NOW!`

That had been sent last night, right after I left the bar.

`I'm freaking out. Please let me know you're OK.`

Guilt spread through my core. Shelby loved me and wanted what was best for me, but I'd tossed her caution aside like it meant nothing. I didn't regret it, though. Last night had been my own little slice of heaven. Being in Danny's arms and feeling the intimacy of his touch had been salve to my lonely heart. His arms around me, his lips intoxicating me, had caused me to forget everything else but him.

My heart felt like it was tearing itself in two. I wanted to trust my best friend, but I needed Danny. Her attempt to help had ripped some major wounds open for both Danny and me.

In the end, it pushed us closer at lightning speed, and I couldn't be mad at her for that.

`Just seeing these. Sorry to worry you. I'm okay.`

What if Shelby told people about what she found on the Internet? Last night, Danny had said one of the reasons he'd left Redding was that everyone looked at him like some sort of lowlife woman-beater after he got out of jail. He didn't need that here, too.

My phone dinged.

`Where have you been? You scared the crap out of me!`

How was I going to convince her that Danny wasn't a bad guy?

`Sorry, can we get together today before work? We need to talk.`

Hopefully, she'd kept her mouth shut about her little Internet revelation.

`Meet me at Midway's at 10:30 for Charlie's breakfast special.`

I checked my watch. That didn't give me much time, but I had to talk to her before she told anyone.

`See you there.`

After taking a quick shower, I threw on my work uniform and pulled my hair into a loose ponytail. I put on a bit of concealer around my eyes to hide the evidence of how little sleep I'd gotten over the last few nights, brushed on some mascara, and headed out the door.

When I slipped into Midway's, Shelby was at the bar, a

mimosa in front of her. "So, what's the scoop with Danny?" I overheard her ask Charlie as I crept up behind her. "What kind of scumbag puts his hands on a pregnant woman?"

Charlie's stance was immediately defensive. "Not all the gossip you hear is true."

"It wasn't gossip," Shelby snapped back. "I found it on a legitimate site on the Internet."

A part of me wanted to hear the rest of the conversation before Shelby saw me, but Charlie had already noticed I'd come in. "Hey guys."

Shelby spun around, bolted up, and threw her arms around me. "Girl. I'm so glad you're okay. You scared me to death."

I couldn't hold back the smile that overtook my face. I was more than okay.

"Oh, wow." She looked over at Charlie, who was busy with the guys at the end of the bar. She grabbed me by the elbow and pulled me to a quiet corner. "You slept with him, didn't you?"

My smile grew. She would hate me, but I couldn't hide it. Might as well own it. "It's wrong to kiss and tell, isn't it?"

Shelby's upper lip curled in revulsion. "What in the Sam Hill is wrong with you? Did you not read that paper? Danny isn't just a bad guy, he's a scum-of-the-earth creeper. A real-life psychopath, and you go and sleep with him?" Her words had started out hushed, but the last line seemed like she'd screamed it at the top of her lungs.

"Shh." I glanced around.

Charlie's gaze was on us. Something strange crept over his face, and he quickly averted his eyes.

Heat tinged my cheeks. I'd figured this would be her response, but she could have at least been respectful about it. I didn't want the whole town knowing my business. "You don't understand, Danny is innocent."

Shelby narrowed her eyes and crossed her arms in front of

her. "*Sure*, he is."

How could I convince her she was believing a lie? Charlie was Danny's cousin. Maybe he would help explain that Danny wasn't a horrible person. "Come on." I pulled her back to the bar.

She plopped back down on the stool and took a long swallow of her mimosa. A drink sounded really good. Anything to take the edge off this conversation would be nice. If I didn't have to work in less than a half hour, I would have ordered one. I waved Charlie over.

He came close and leaned against the bar. That look in his eyes was there again. What in the world was it?

"Will you please tell Shelby the truth about Danny? She won't believe me that he's innocent."

He looked back and forth between me and Shelby, seeming to consider what he should say. "Innocent regarding what?"

"Don't mess around, Charlie. We don't need any of your head games. Don't be butt-sore because Tamara's into Danny."

He threw her a disgusted look. "Shut up, Shelby."

"Guys, come on." I said. "We're simply after the truth. Did his ex screw him over because he didn't want to be with her anymore?"

Charlie leaned against the bar with both hands. "It's complicated, but yes. Danny may be a lot of things, but he'd never hit a woman. He was raised better than that."

I cocked my head to the side. *Danny may be a lot of things?* What was that supposed to mean? He must have been referring to the cheating, but that wasn't fair. The way Danny made it sound, he and Marisa were practically broken up. Did Charlie not believe Danny? Was Charlie the one who'd told Danny he wasn't good enough for me? After last night, the past didn't matter anymore. I would never treat him like Marisa had. I would always encourage him to follow his dreams.

I turned to Shelby. "Please just be happy for me. I've never felt anything like this before." That was a bold statement to make in front of Charlie, but a part of me wanted the whole world to know.

Her countenance softened. "I'm only looking out for you. I was really freaked out when I saw that online. He was proven guilty in a court of law."

"I promise you, Shelby. I don't want Tamara getting hurt either," Charlie said. "The charges were totally fabricated. Her best friend told me after the trial was over. Danny isn't perfect, but what she did was completely messed up."

"You keep saying Danny's not perfect. If he didn't hit her, what *did* he do?" Shelby said.

"He cheated on her." Charlie wasn't dancing around it. I might as well get it out in the open and deal with the backlash.

"No wonder she freaked out." Shelby's voice went up an octave.

"They had a horrible relationship and were on the verge of breaking up." I turned to Charlie and shot him a look. I needed his support.

"Do you hear yourself right now?" Shelby's glare felt lethal.

My pleading gaze landed on her. Why couldn't she be happy for me?

"You mark my words, Tamara, people don't change."

I glanced at Charlie to see his reaction to Shelby's last words. His expression seemed uneasy. Was there more to the story? "What is it?"

"I just don't want to see you get hurt." Charlie paused for a moment, seeming to choose his words carefully. "Have you ever thought about praying about it?"

"Seriously?" Shelby huffed. "When did you become all religious?"

Charlie's cheeks flushed. "I'm not, okay?" He picked up a

glass next to him and polished it with a towel. "It's just something I've been thinking about lately."

"Well, if there is a God out there, he could care less about me or Tamara. Or even you, for that matter," she spat out, bitterness lacing her tone.

Ouch. She didn't have to be so harsh. But in some ways, I agreed with her. When I was a young child, I'd believed in a loving God, but that was before my prayers were never answered and everything I cared about was taken away.

"Hey, you guys. I gotta go." I jumped off the barstool and gave Shelby a hug. "Thank you for caring so much." I glanced back at Charlie as I walked to the door. "And thank you for your advice. I'll think about it." I probably wouldn't, but I wanted to make him feel better after the way Shelby had treated him. If nothing else, his sentiment had been sweet.

Charlie's mouth tilted up a bit. "You have a good day."

"Thanks. You too," I said and walked out the door.

July 4, 8:47 p.m. – Tamara

People don't change … Shelby's words haunted me all throughout my shift and into the evening. Danny had invited me to come over the night before, but I was emotionally spent and exhausted. I went home, slept and worked the next day, the whole time my emotions on edge about Danny.

Was Shelby right? When I was with Danny, I felt so sure. His charm and sweetness were impossible to resist. Now that he wasn't near enough for me to feel the electrical connection radiating between us, Shelby's words echoed in my mind and felt awfully convincing. And Charlie hadn't done much to put me at ease.

There was a light knock at my door. I was supposed to meet Shelby down at the beach in half an hour to watch the fireworks. I texted Danny earlier and invited him, but he didn't like the idea of hanging with Shelby. I guess I couldn't blame him.

I opened the door.

Danny stood in front of me, smiling, hair falling over his face. "Hey, angel." He came through the door, put his arms around me, and kissed me deeply, hungrily. We lost ourselves for a few minutes before he pulled away. "Sorry to just stop by. I really missed you."

His arms around me were the best thing I'd felt since seeing him last. So strong but so gentle. Saying I'd missed him didn't seem like an intense enough word. I kissed him again with the same fervor, my lips communicating what words couldn't.

My phone rang, and I groaned. Shelby was probably wondering where I was. I pulled away to answer it, but by the time I found it at the bottom of my purse, she'd hung up. "It's Shelby," I told Danny.

His gaze flitted toward the floor.

"She's probably wondering where I am."

Danny put his arms around me once more. "That's actually why I'm here."

"What?"

His lips twitched as if he was trying to hold back a smile. "I'm here to kidnap you for the night. Just you, not Shelby."

I squirmed a bit. "Come on, Danny, she was only trying to protect me."

Sadness overshadowed his face. "But I almost lost you."

I wrapped my arms around his neck. "But you didn't. If anything, it pushed us closer together faster. Now, we know each other's secrets, and we're both still here."

"That doesn't change anything with her and me."

"She's my best friend."

His face came close to mine. "I'm not trying to be a jerk. I'll work on forgiving her. I'm not there yet, though."

I sighed. "That's fair."

"Please come with me tonight? I have something special planned." Those eyes... How could I resist?

Shelby wouldn't be happy if I bailed on her, but if things were reversed, she'd probably ditch me. My phone rang again, but this time, I ignored it on purpose and shot her a quick text, telling her I wasn't feeling well and to have fun without me. Guilt nudged me in the stomach, but she had Nick and the rest of the gang. She wouldn't miss me too much.

"Where are we going?" I asked.

A huge smile broke over Danny's face. "Like I said, it's a surprise." He offered me his hand.

I took it and followed him. His guitar was leaning against the wall outside my door. The sun was just setting, and the sky was painted in beautiful strokes of pinks and purples. Sounds of kids lighting firecrackers and bottle rockets filled the air. He picked up his guitar and pulled me toward the ocean.

"Danny, we can't go to the beach. Shelby's down there." I abruptly stopped. If she caught me blowing her off to be with Danny, I'd never hear the end of it.

"Just trust me." He tugged my hand. I followed him down an alleyway that led in a direction I'd never been before. "I'll be careful," he assured me.

When we finally made it to the beach, the place was crowded. Shelby was nowhere in sight, which eased the anxiety in my stomach. Danny navigated me through pockets of people, gathering to watch the fireworks show. The area was full of lawn chairs, blankets, and kids running around.

"How about over there?" He pointed just away from the shoreline, behind some driftwood.

It didn't look as comfortable as the smooth beach, but it was more secluded. "Looks great."

He led me over the gathering of logs, branches, and other random pieces of driftwood. I failed to keep my balance a couple of times, but Danny's strong arm helped keep me centered. After a little navigation, we came to a nice little pocket of sand that had a blanket, a couple of candles, and a thermos.

"You already had this set up?" Stunned, I smacked his arm playfully.

"Guilty." He sat down and motioned me to the blanket.

"What if I had turned you down and went with Shelby instead?" I joined him on the blanket.

"Then I would have just drowned my sorrows in this Silver Oak Cabernet alone." He opened the thermos.

"Are you crazy?"

He flashed an innocent smile and raised his hand to his chest. "Whatever do you mean?"

"First of all, that's a ninety-nine-dollar bottle of wine."

"Nothing but the best for my lady." He dipped his head toward me in a slight bow.

I didn't know if I should kiss him or punch him. I wanted to do both. "And you're not supposed to have alcohol on the beach."

"I won't tell if you don't. I broke open the best bottle of wine Charlie had for this special occasion." He handed me the container.

"Expensive wine from a plastic thermos, real smooth."

He winked and his mouth pursed into a half-smile. "I thought we already covered this on our first date. King of Class, remember?"

"What is the special occasion?" I took a sip of the very expensive wine. It was nice, though, red wasn't usually my thing.

"Besides Independence Day? I finished a new song and want to play it for you." Leaning back, he opened his guitar case. He picked it up and put the strap over his shoulder. Placing one hand on the neck of the guitar, he pressed down and finger-plucked with the other hand, creating a beautiful melody.

"I was born in an American town
where the mountains touch the face of God
and she was born on the wrong side of the tracks."

The light of the candles flickered over his face as he sang. It was beautiful. *He* was beautiful. If I could have paused that moment and stayed there forever, I would have been the happiest woman alive.

"One night, she came into my arms.
She said, 'I've been through hell, but you can take what's left."

The words resounded deep in my heart. I *had* been through hell, and though I hadn't told him the gory details, somehow, he'd picked up on what was between the hazy lines.

"What's left of that girl is a fallen angel,
what's left is a fallen angel,
what's left is a chance of a new life in the arms of this cowboy.
What's left is a will to carry on when
you thought your life was over.
What's left is a fallen angel for me, just for me."

The other night, when we were making love, I didn't think I could fall any harder for this mysterious man, but now, I realized I was so wrong. The words of the song and the way he sang them to me were insanely exhilarating. Every fiber of my being was his, and from the way he sang, I knew he was all mine.

"She wrapped me in her arms like a lover
And slowly closed my eyes so I could see.
The beauty of her world and all its wonder,
she showed to me, she gave to me."

He finished strumming the last chord and set the guitar aside. His eyes had been on me the entire song. Kneeling in front of me, his expression held an intensity that was hard to look away from. "There's something I'd like to ask you."

"Anything." My mind was still swirling around the song and the emotions it had stirred in me.

"Tamara Christine Jensen." He took hold of both my hands. "We've only known each other for a few short weeks, but last night, when you weren't in my arms, it was like there was a crevasse the size of the Grand Canyon inside my soul."

He certainly had a way with words, but was he being sincere? His eyes told me he was. It was possible that I was being played by this beautiful man in front of me, but everything in me wanted to believe he meant what he said.

"You're going to think I'm absolutely crazy, but I want you to move in with me."

All the air was sucked out of my lungs. Move in with him? He was more than crazy—he was completely insane! I stood and took a few steps away to a large patch of sand grass. He was immediately behind me, his hand touching my back.

"I know it's a lot so soon, but after what you told me about your ex, I just think you'd be safer with me." He moved closer and pulled my hair away from my neck. His lips made soft trails on the back of it. "I couldn't handle it if anything happened to you."

His breath on my skin caused shivers to run down my spine. Or was it his words? I turned around. My eyes were filled with tears as I looked up at him. "Are you for real?"

"One hundred and fifty percent." Above us, several mortars exploded, lighting up the night sky. Danny's lips quirked up a little. "Just like the movies. Except they were supposed to go off when I was kissing you. But maybe this is the more appropriate moment." He wove his fingers through mine. "Just say yes," he whispered.

My mind ran through all the reasons I shouldn't and caught the biggest one. Shelby. She had tried to get me to move in with her six months ago, but I'd refused. I hadn't wanted to leave her in a lurch if I had to leave town in the middle of the night. This, with Danny, was different. He knew about the possible risk. More than that, he wanted to protect me.

"Shelby is going to freak out."

More fireworks exploded, streaking the sky with green, red, and blue.

"Why do you care so much about what she thinks? You act like she owns you or something."

I pulled away, suddenly frustrated. "That's not fair."

Danny grabbed my arm. "Hey, I'm sorry. I didn't mean that."

A gust of wind blew around us. The candles flickered as if they might go out. "I hate that you guys can't stand each other."

His eyes softened. "I promise, Tamara, I will try with Shelby. Even after what she did." He pulled me in close to him. "For you." His head rested on mine.

My eyes landed on the blanket, thermos, and wine. Then the guitar. A strange, intoxicating feeling fell over me. He wanted this. He wanted *me*. "You promise?"

"I'll do anything. Just move in with me."

My whole body seemed to hum with the idea of waking up in his arms every morning, but there was one thing that didn't make sense. "What's in it for you?"

"What do you mean?"

"You want to keep me safe, but what do *you* get out of it?"

He was quiet for a long moment, his gaze lingering on my face. "You don't understand. Before we met, I was dying on the inside. Things were so broken, I didn't know how to move forward. Being with you …" His hands ran over my hips and then up my back. "Being with you helps me believe again. Being with you makes me feel alive."

His lips met mine. He made me feel more than alive. He made me feel powerful and euphoric. My hands wound their way up his neck and through his dark hair. There was nothing in me that could tell him no. It didn't matter what Shelby would say. I'd give Danny whatever he asked if it meant I could have more of him.

July 6, 4:32 p.m. – Tamara

"Are you out of your mind?" Shelby's mouth dropped open, her face red. "Tamara, you met him three weeks ago. You can't just move in with him."

I placed a stack of books in a box next to the bed. She was absolutely right on so many levels, but for some reason, I couldn't tell him no. It was as if he'd cast some sort of love spell on me. There was no way I'd ever be able to explain to her the words he'd spoken to me. The song he'd written for me. The way he'd held me and called me his angel.

I'd never had a guy treat me like Danny did, and I was starving for more of it. "The way things are going, I'd be at his house almost every night anyway."

Shelby glared at me. "Then what's the rush? Don't you want the freedom of having your own place?"

"I think I'll enjoy being in his arms every night more."

She grimaced as if the thought repulsed her. "What if he's lying about everything? Charlie could be lying, too."

I folded my favorite shirt and stuffed it into an overnight bag. "I'm one hundred percent sure that is not happening." If she only knew the tender way he touched me, she would believe him, too.

"What if things don't work out with you two? What if he

and his ex get back together, and he leaves you high and dry?"

"Then I guess I'll be crashing at your place." If things didn't work out with Danny, I'd be leaving town, but that wasn't something I was ready to tell her. I didn't want to think like that, but if there was one thing I had learned, it was to have a plan B. Besides, living with Danny would allow me to save more money.

She let out an exasperated sigh and threw her hands in the air. "Talking to you right now is obviously a waste of breath. I'll just have to take matters up with Danny." She stormed out of my apartment before I could say another word.

My heart rate doubled at the thought of what she might do. But a good confrontation might be what they both needed. I finished packing the bag I'd been working on, then followed after Shelby.

July 6, 5:02 p.m. – Danny

Just as I stepped out of the shower stall, someone pounded on the front door with such intensity, it sounded like a cop conducting door-to-door searches. I fastened a towel around my waist, quickly made my way to the door, and opened it.

Shelby stood in front of me.

My stomach wound into a massive knot. After what she'd pulled with me and Tamara, avoiding her for the next ten years had been the plan.

"Can I help you?" I said coolly, though my insides were anything but cool. This was the woman who was trying to keep me away from Tamara. My number one enemy.

Her eyes raked me from head to toe.

Was she checking me out? This chick was something else.

"Actually, yes." She pushed past me into *my* dwelling. "You can explain to me why you feel the need to take advantage of my best friend."

Take advantage? Man, she had some nerve. My hands balled into fists.

"You think you can just waltz into town, sing a few songs, and sweep her off her feet?" Her voice grew louder. "'cause I don't buy it for one second. What's your *real* motive, Danny?"

"I can't pretend to know what you're talking about," I said

through clenched teeth. "But I don't remember inviting you into my house. So, why don't you get out?"

"Not until I get some answers." She walked over and poked my bare chest. "Tamara says those charges weren't true, but why should I believe that?"

I'd never wanted to hit a woman so badly in my life. "What do you want me to say?" I grabbed her hand and flung it away. "Do you know what it's like to have lies made up about you? And then go to jail for something you would never do? Oh, how about having someone withhold the rights to your child because they want to mess with your life?" I was yelling now.

She cowered a bit.

I took in a deep breath to rein in the rage. "Listen, Shelby, I guess I don't care if you believe me or not, but what I *do* know is that Tamara *does*. When I'm with her, that stuff doesn't hurt so much. It's like she's healing me."

Her expression softened a bit, but she kept quiet.

"I came here to get away from the past. I don't need it thrown in my face every time I turn around, so please stop bringing it up."

She averted her eyes and swallowed hard.

Had I gotten through to her?

"Just don't hurt her." She bolted out the door as abruptly as she'd come.

Through the door, I could see Tamara come up the walkway. Not good. She'd never seen me this worked up before.

Shelby paused, then stormed past Tamara.

I tried to regain my composure as Tamara walked through the door and closed it. "Wow, she was pissed." Her eyes held a bit of concern, but her mouth twitched like she was holding back a smile. "Everything okay?"

"I would never hit a girl, but I wanted to punch that one."

Tamara laughed and moved closer to me. "I'm pretty sure

she wanted to punch you too. She's not happy with this." She took my hand. "What did she say?"

My hand curled around hers. "She said not to hurt you."

"Well, she's right, you better not hurt me, Danny." She winked and flashed a flirtatious grin. "I'm sorry, though, I can't take you seriously with so few clothes on."

"Oh, yeah?"

"Yeah." She pushed my chest.

I pulled her close, wrapping my arms around her waist. "Well, maybe we need to get you into my bedroom and even the playing field."

"Don't you mean *our* bedroom?"

I could feel myself smile bigger than the Cheshire cat. This beautiful girl had been like a drug—the kind that helped me forget everything that was wrong with my world, and now, she was going to be living with me. I'd be able to kiss her every morning and hold her every night.

Picking her up, I carried her into our bedroom and shut the door behind us.

September 13, 8:45 p.m. – Tamara

The first couple months of living with Danny were wonderful, full of laughter, music, and passion. Most evenings were spent on the beach with a campfire and Danny playing his guitar. Shelby and Nick would even join us sometimes. It had still been a bit uncomfortable between Shelby and Danny, but they'd had no big blowups like they'd had during those first few weeks.

Everything was mostly perfect, but tonight felt different. I returned home from work to thrasher music blaring from the backyard. I walked around the back to see Danny sitting in a lawn chair, a half-empty fifth of Jack Daniels in one hand, a cigarette in the other.

"There's my angel." His mouth twisted into a mocking smile.

A sick feeling slithered around my stomach. Something was seriously wrong. I walked across the patio to the stereo and turned it down.

"Hey! I was listening to that!" He yelled through a slur.

"So was the whole neighborhood," I said, voice hushed. "What's going on?"

He narrowed his eyes and sucked in a large drag. "What could possibly be going on?" He exhaled, raised his hands in the air, and looked up into the sky. "I live in this beautiful paradise with my gorgeous girlfriend." He stood and wobbled a bit. "No, I'm great. I'm just celebrating."

"Celebrating?"

His eyebrows pinched together scornfully. "Did you forget already, angel?"

My mind went blank. His birthday wasn't until November.

"Today, at 3:44 p.m., I became a father to a baby boy I'll never meet." He took a large swig of whiskey.

My heart sank. When we'd gotten together, he'd said his ex was six months pregnant. Sometimes the topic would come up, and he'd get this faraway look in his eye, but then he would just shrug it off, and I never pressed him.

"Oh, Danny, I'm so sorry." I should have realized how much this was consuming him. How could I have been so oblivious?

"Don't give me that. You didn't even know what I was talking about." He took a drag off the cigarette and flicked it onto the ground. "I swear, you women are all the same," he muttered under his breath.

His words struck my heart like a spear. "How could you say that? I would never do anything like what she did to you."

His eyes deepened, and the pain in them was more than I could bear.

I crouched down next to him and took his hand in mine.

He closed his eyes and tears fell down his cheeks. "You don't understand what I've done. Or who I am, Tamara. I deserve every bit of what she's done to me." He slammed back more of the Jack.

The volume of what he was drinking was really freaking me out. "Nobody deserves what she's doing to you."

"I'll never be good enough for my child, and I'll never be good enough for you."

"Please stop this." I took the bottle out of his hand. "I don't know about that other life you had. We've both had crazy lives so far, but you don't have to stay there. What matters is that we're here now. We have each other. Can't that be enough?"

He jerked back his hand and stood, anger flaring in his eyes. "I'm sorry, but it's not. You can't make me forget my child!"

"I don't want you to forget!" I raised my voice as I stood.

"That's what it sounds like!" Danny shouted.

"You're twisting my words!"

"Am I?" Danny sneered and then walked toward the house. "I don't need this!"

I followed after him. "What are you doing?"

"What does it look like. I'm going for a walk. I need some air."

"Please don't leave like this. You're scaring me." I was trembling.

"Sorry, princess. I guess you don't get your fairytale life after all. None of us do." He stormed out the door, and it slammed behind him.

My heart split down the middle, filled with helplessness and defeat. I wanted to run after him. To beg him to come back, but in that moment, I was too scared of what I'd just seen. What if he turned that anger toward me? What if he'd been lying to me this whole time? I tried to swallow back the tears that were threatening to come.

No, I *knew* Danny. He was just drunk and angry. And he had every reason to be. The best thing to do now was give him space. He'd cool down and be back to his normal self in a few hours.

At least, I hoped he would.

September 13, 9:22 p.m. – Danny

There wasn't enough whiskey in the world to numb the agony in my chest. Fighting with Tamara had only made it worse. Maybe I could head up to the casino and mouth off to some moron, just so I could pound the crap out of something. I walked about five minutes in that direction, when a couple of headlights pulled up beside me and the driver rolled down the passenger window.

"Need a ride?"

I ducked down.

Shelby was in the driver's seat.

Interesting.

I would have expected her to run me over, not offer me a ride. I thought about how long a walk to the casino would be and figured, *why not?* What was the worst that could happen? "I'm heading to the casino."

She raised one of her perfectly-shaped eyebrows. "That's kind of a long walk, isn't it?"

I shrugged nonchalantly. Shelby didn't need to know how jacked up I was on the inside. That was none of her business. "I need to clear my head."

"Trouble in paradise?" Her head tilted a little as if she were offering a listening ear.

"Something like that." There was no way I could trust her with the details of this saga. But a ride would be nice.

"Well, don't just stand there. Get in."

Without further thought, I lifted the handle on Shelby's mid-nineties Mustang and got in.

She wore a skin-tight, black mini-skirt that showed way more of her flawless legs than it covered, and a halter top that left little to the imagination.

"Nice outfit." I took another glance at her barely-clothed body. Did she have to put so much on display? "Were you on your way to a date with Nick?" Man, I needed more alcohol. Small talk with my archenemy wasn't lessening the pain.

She pulled out a cigarette and rolled down the window. "Nick's working. I'm bored. Figured I'd hit Midway's."

"You're going out on the town dressed like that without your boyfriend?" What a dumb thing to say. Hopefully, she wouldn't kick me out of the car.

"What of it?" She pressed hard on the gas pedal.

"It's just that when a guy sees a girl dressed like that at a bar with no boyfriend at her side, he's probably thinking one thing."

"Oh, yeah?" The tone of her voice felt flirtatious. "What exactly would that be?"

"That she's putting out the bait. Trying to reel in a big stud to take her home and show her what's up."

She giggled a seductive little laugh. "Or maybe she just likes the free drinks it gets her."

"Touché." I chuckled. Was I actually enjoying myself with Shelby? Maybe she wasn't as terrible as I had thought.

A few minutes later, we pulled into the parking lot of the casino. "Can I buy you a drink for bringing me out here?"

She looked me up and down. "Does this mean all is forgiven? Can we actually be friends after everything?"

I gave her a tentative smile. "Why not?"

She grinned back. "That's kinda lame, but I'll take the drink."

Making nice with Shelby would probably be the best thing I could do for my relationship with Tamara. I cringed at the thought of her name. Why had I been such a jerk to her during our fight? Why couldn't I just let her comfort me?

Because deep down, I knew I'd never deserve her love.

A guy like me deserved a woman more like Shelby. Nothing serious, just casual fun. And that's what I needed tonight—to drink a ton more booze, have fun, and forget the pain.

September 13, 11:16 p.m. – Tamara

After Danny left, I did something I hadn't done in years. I prayed. I prayed for Danny, that God would keep him safe. I prayed that God would heal his wounded heart and that He would bring him home to me soon because I was worried sick.

Several times, I tried calling him, but he never answered. I tried praying again but felt hopeless. I tried writing in my journal, but that didn't help. All my fears came rushing out onto the paper, yet instead of releasing them, the act only amplified them, as if writing them down gave them more power.

I ripped the paper out of the book and shredded it into a hundred small pieces.

Finally, I decided to walk up to Midway's to see if he was there. If he was, would he be more belligerently drunk? Or would he let me help him home, so I could put him to bed and hope this would blow over in the morning? Icicles formed in my stomach. What if our relationship so far had been a facade? Would I be able to survive if Danny broke my heart? I shook my head. This was only a fight after a very hard day for him. Tomorrow, we could start over fresh. His words had hurt me, but I could easily forgive him. I just needed to find him and get him home.

Walking into Midway's, I scanned the crowd. A few people

milled around the dartboard. Two couples were playing teams at the pool table. The bar itself was mostly full, and Charlie was behind the counter, free-pouring a shot of tequila.

But there was no Danny.

I walked up to the bar and waited impatiently for Charlie to come tend to me. There were three other customers ahead of me, so it took way longer than I cared for.

"Hey, Tamara." His smile was a bit too—I don't know—happy? Friendly? Eager? "What can I get for you?"

I swallowed the lump forming in my throat. "I don't need anything. I'm just wondering if you've seen Danny."

His smile quickly faded. "Nope, the last time I saw him in here was with you."

I bit the inside of my cheek, trying to suppress the emotion that threatened to overtake me. "Okay. Thanks, anyway."

His eyebrows pinched together. "What's going on?"

"Danny became a father today." My throat constricted around the words.

"I know. I called him this afternoon with the news."

"How did you know?"

He leaned in close and spoke quietly. "Marisa called me afterwards." Something dark shadowed Charlie's eyes. "She told me she didn't even put Danny's name on the birth certificate."

"Wow …" How vindictive could this woman be? No wonder Danny had been so broken. What more could she do to him? She had already stolen three months of his life, destroyed his reputation, and now, this. "That makes a lot more sense."

Confusion settled over Charlie's features. "What do you mean?"

"When I came home from work this evening, he was completely drunk. I could tell he was broken and angry, but this is worse. Will she ever be done punishing him?"

"There's not much more she can do."

"I'm really worried about him. He picked a fight with me and took off." I checked the clock on my phone. "He's been gone for almost two hours."

Charlie didn't say anything, but something peculiar crept over his face.

What was it? Suspicion? Anger? Either way, I didn't have time to figure it out. "I'm going to go look for him."

"Hey, Charlie." A patron called from across the bar. "I need another beer. Make it a Bud this time."

"Coming right up." Charlie leaned in again. "I don't get off until 2 a.m. I'll let you know if he comes in."

"Thanks. I'll text you if I find him." I turned away from the bar.

"Oh, and Tamara? I'll say a prayer for him."

I gave him a sad smile before turning toward the door. Maybe his prayers would work better than mine had. Darkness crashed over my soul as I walked out of the bar. Where was Danny? Something in me felt infinitely lost as I set out to find him.

September 13, 11:20 p.m. – Danny

"Jägerbomb!" Shelby's eyes lit up like a kid going on her first ride at Disneyland.

The whole world was a haze. There was no more pain—only the ecstasy of numbness. We'd already had three shots each and shared a pitcher of beer. "Sounds like a spectacular idea." I threw my arm around her shoulder to steady myself. "But I have one question. Aren't you the DD?" Oh man, I could hear the slur in my own speech. Pathetic.

She slid her arm around my waist and pushed her body into mine. "We can get a cab and pick my car up tomorrow. Right now, I want to partaaay." She raised her other hand in the air and waved it back and forth.

"Hot damn, girl, let's get you another round." I waved down the bartender and ordered us a couple of Jägerbombs.

When the bartender handed us the drinks, Shelby lifted hers in the air. "How 'bout a toast?"

"I got one." I lifted my glass in the air. "To forgetting the past, and to giving the future a big middle finger. Screw them both. Let's live in the now."

Shelby burst out laughing. "For a songwriter, I would have expected something a bit more eloquent, but I'll drink to that."

"Come on, now. Give me a break. I'm at least a half a fifth

ahead of you."

"Then I'll just have to catch up." She clicked her glass against mine, then we both shot them back.

Hanging out with Shelby was surprisingly fun. I liked how she could cut loose and be lighthearted. I couldn't see Tamara being like that. If I was with her right now, we would probably be talking through my "feelings" and crap like that. For the moment, those feelings were too damn raw to be attended to. Fun was the best medicine. Never would've thought that I'd prefer Shelby's company to Tamara's. Not in a million decades.

Sam Smith's "Stay with Me" came over the speakers, and Shelby's eyes lit up. Swaying her hips to the music, she ran her hands seductively over her own curves.

She was way too hot for her own good. And with every shot, she became more attractive.

She ran a finger down my chest, and heat pulsed through me. "Come dance with me." She tugged me toward the dance floor.

"I'm too drunk for that." I laughed.

She ran her hands up my chest, down my arm, and then wove her fingers through mine. "This is a slow song. Just follow my lead and go easy."

As much as I hated myself for it, I liked the way she felt. The ground wobbled a bit as I followed her out to the dance floor. She placed my hands on each side of her hips, then wrapped her hands around my neck and pressed her body against mine. She sang the lyrics about a one-night stand to me as we swayed to the music. My body reacted intensely to the way hers felt against mine. I looked down at her and our eyes met. Desire rippled through me and then she leaned forward, and our lips met. The next few moments were a blur as we were full-on making out.

"Danny." She pulled away. "We gotta get out of here before

someone sees us."

I swallowed, nodded, and then followed her out to her car, which was parked against a dimly-lit wall.

"I'll drive." I reached for the keys.

"Yeah, right." She laughed, lifting the keys as far away from me as she could. "Didn't you say you were a half a fifth ahead of me?"

"I drive better when I'm drunk." I lunged for the keys and wrestled them out of her hand. Laughing hard, I raised them far above her head.

"*Nobody* drives better drunk." She slid her hands seductively around my neck.

"I do." I kissed her again. "Now, let's get out of here."

September 14, 5:34 a.m. – Danny

My throbbing head felt like someone had bashed me with a sledgehammer several times. Those first few moments of consciousness, all I could feel was the nausea tearing at my stomach and the pounding in my skull. Then memories of last night came pouring through my mind—one excruciating scene after the next. The fight with Tamara, doing shots with Shelby at the bar, her dragging me onto the dance floor, kissing, and then us in the back of her car.

Nausea tightened my stomach. No. No. No. Those memories couldn't be real. This was a horrible nightmare. I sat up and looked around.

I was in the back of Shelby's car, parked in the middle of nowhere. My head throbbed. That meant that one of us drove last night. Neither of us should have.

Shelby was passed out, her face smashed against the back window. Pure, unadulterated guilt pressed down on me, so hard it knocked the air out of my lungs.

This was probably the worst thing I'd done in my life. I hadn't started cheating on Marissa until our relationship was close to being over. Tamara and I were just beginning. She was only trying to comfort me last night, and I ran off and did *this*—with her best friend, of all people. The betrayal of it was too much for anyone to take. Tamara could never know. It would kill her.

Shelby stirred, groaned, then bolted up. She looked at me, face ashen. "What did we do?" She put her head between her legs. "What in the hell did we do, Danny?"

I put my hand on her back but felt weird about comforting her. She was right to freak out.

Eyes wild, she looked up at me. "You can't tell her. Please don't tell her," she begged. "She'll hate both of us."

"I know." I could only hope that nobody had seen us. Guilt twisted my stomach harder as the sun shone through the car window.

Tamara was probably sick with worry.

How was I going to face her after this? I reached for my phone that was lying on the floorboard. As I picked up the phone and looked at it, a shock of panic jolted through my body.

Sometime in the middle of the night, I had butt-dialed Charlie.

What if he'd heard me and Shelby? If he knew, then there was no way to hide this horrific thing from Tamara.

I had promised her I wouldn't break her heart, but this might actually shatter it.

September 14, 6:17 a.m. – Tamara

I checked my phone for the hundredth time. Still no word from Danny. My eyes burned from tears that wouldn't stop, and my mind went through a thousand different what-ifs. What if he decided to wade into the ocean and got lost in an undertow? What if he stumbled in front of a moving vehicle and was in the hospital? What if he went and picked a bar fight and was in jail? What if he found comfort in the arms of another woman? For hours, my mind conjured up the most gruesome images, taunting me in the cruelest of ways.

I had searched for him until one-thirty in the morning, to no avail. I had gone to every establishment within walking distance and searched up and down the beach, but he wasn't there. Eventually, I went home to cry myself to sleep.

Sleep never came.

I rolled over in bed and punched a pillow, tears streaming down my face. What had I gotten myself into with Danny? I should have left town before I'd given him my heart.

The front door creaked open and my body went rigid. Was it finally him?

Light footsteps crossed the floor. Then his hand was on my back, sliding around my stomach.

I turned over to see his face.

His eyes were tortured, his expression full of remorse.

"Where were you?" I said with equal parts anger and relief.

He shook his head. "The last thing I remember was our fight last night and storming out like a complete jerk. And then I woke up a couple of miles down the beach." Tears spilled over his eyes. "I'm so sorry, Tamara. You have no idea how sorry I am."

Tears ran down my cheeks, too, and he brushed them away with his thumb.

"Oh, beautiful girl, I know I hurt you. Please forgive me."

"You really freaked me out. I searched for you until one-thirty in the morning."

"I'm here now, and I'm not going anywhere." He wrapped his arms around me and pulled me close. "Unless you want me to."

I buried my head into his chest. The smell of alcohol and … what was it? A familiar, sweet, musky smell. Something niggled at my brain. Maybe my mind was conjuring up something because he'd disappeared for so long. A part of me wanted to confront him, but another part just wanted this fight to be over. For his arms to be wrapped around me. To make this ache in my chest go away.

"I don't want you to leave. I only want you to quit punishing yourself for the past. I know I could never take the place of what you lost. But I want to build a future with you."

He pulled my face up. "I'll never be worthy of you, but I'll sure try."

"Trying is what matters, Danny." I rested my head back on his chest. Though a part of me was still angry with him for putting me through this, the comfort of his arms and knowing he was safe eased the tension in my body. Listening to the soft rhythm of his heart, I surrendered to his embrace.

September 17, 11:30 a.m. – Tamara

Over the next three days, things were different between Danny and me. He'd come to bed way later than I did, then sleep past the time I went to work.

This morning, when I woke up, Danny wasn't next to me. I looked around the house, but he was nowhere. Would things ever go back to the way they were before? Since he'd come home the morning after our fight, there'd been an invisible wall between us. Though he'd been mostly sweet and kind to me, there was an overall feeling of distance and coldness. As if he was stuck in the pain of what Marisa had done to him and out of my reach.

I walked out to the front deck and lit up a cigarette.

Danny was down at the ocean, pacing back and forth, waving his hands around as if he were having an intense conversation with someone who wasn't there. This thing with his son was doing a serious number on him. There had to be some way to help.

I flicked away the ash and took another drag. Maybe I should go down there? He looked pretty emotional, though, and he hadn't reacted well when I had tried to be there for him. There were some things one had to face alone. No one understood that more than me.

After taking a few more drags, I snuffed out the smoke in the ashtray. It was time to get ready for work.

Back inside, I took a long shower and tried not to worry about Danny, but it was impossible. How could I help him fight this all-consuming depression? I dried off, brushed my teeth, and blow-dried my hair.

While doing my makeup, I heard the door open and close. I forced myself not to rush through brushing on my mascara. I calmly walked out of the bathroom and expected to see him sitting on the couch, but he wasn't there. I checked the bedroom.

Empty. Had I imagined the sound of the door? Leaving the room, I noticed him in the backyard, on a lawn chair, his back to me.

Anxiety tightened my stomach. I checked my watch. I had a few minutes before I needed to leave. Maybe I should sneak out and leave him alone. Taking in a deep breath, I berated myself for being such a coward and started toward Danny. I stopped at the door and watched him through the small window. His shoulders drooped and there seemed to be a blanket of despair that shrouded him. He lifted a flask to his mouth and took a large swallow.

Tears stung my eyes. Not quite noon and he was already drinking? I didn't know whether to go out and yell at him or call in sick and babysit him.

Either way, this could end very badly.

I pushed open the door, walked over to him, and put my hand on his shoulder. "Hey, sweetie, I'm heading to work."

He looked up at me, eyes red and puffy. "Okay."

My heart fell into my stomach. What I would give to end his torment. I knelt down and wrapped my arms around him. "I love you, Danny McMillan. Please quit torturing yourself."

He didn't say anything but pulled me into his arms,

embracing me like a drowning man holding a lifeline.

"I could call in sick to work if you need me today," I said after a few minutes of silence.

He shook his head. "No, I need to work through this by myself."

I nodded, my heart in a vise. Not knowing what to say, I tried to pull away.

His grip tightened for a second, and then he let me go.

September 17, 12:42 p.m. – Danny

After watching Tamara leave, I slammed back another shot of whiskey. The last three days had been utter hell. I was in the deepest parts of the netherworld, and Satan himself had me chained up, standing over me with a searing pitchfork.

Every time I looked at Tamara, I'd see what I had done, and all-consuming guilt would suffocate me. There had been at least six times my confession was on the tip of my tongue. That morning had been the worst. When she'd told me she loved me, there were such intense, conflicting emotions inside me, sparring with each other. Everything in me wanted to say it back because despite everything, I was sure I did love her. If I didn't, guilt wouldn't have me so choked that most moments, I couldn't breathe when I was with her. I absolutely despised myself for not being the man she needed me to be. Out on the beach this morning, when I was yelling at God for making me like this, I had a revelation.

I had to tell her. She had every right to know the truth and decide for herself what she wanted to do.

Walking into the kitchen, I grabbed my phone and scrolled through the contacts to find Shelby's number and hit the green icon. Shelby had begged me not to tell Tamara what happened because she'd hate both of us, but shouldn't that be Tamara's decision? How in the world did this beautiful angel girl become surrounded by such nasty demons?

"What do you want?" Shelby's voice was low and full of malice.

"Gee, Shelby, good to hear from you, too."

"Hold on a sec." There was silence for a few minutes and a door slammed. "I thought we agreed the other morning not to contact each other."

"Yeah, well, we need to talk."

"I thought we said everything the other morning." Her tone was demeaning and impatient.

"Things have changed since then." I looked at a picture of me and Tamara on the fridge. Her beautiful green eyes were filled with such happiness and trust.

"What did you do, Danny?"

"Nothing yet, but we need to talk alone. Tamara just left for work. Come by as soon as you can." I ran my finger over the picture, my heart screaming at me. This girl loved me so much, and I was about to destroy her.

"Fine." The line went dead.

I poured myself a cup of coffee and added another shot of whiskey, wishing it would quiet the demons.

Lately, nothing helped. The only answer was to confess my sins and pray for mercy. God, I hoped Tamara could forgive me. Maybe then, I could forgive myself.

I rinsed a few dishes that were in the sink and loaded them in the dishwasher.

Shelby knocked at the front door.

I dried my hands before letting her in. "That was quick."

She pushed past me into the living room and swung toward me, eyes blazing with anger. "What kind of game are you playing here?"

"I'm going to tell her." There was no other option. It had

to be done.

She narrowed her eyes. "We already discussed this. We would both lose her. Is that what you want?"

"No, of course not." I exhaled. "But it's killing me. Every time I look at her, all I see is what we did. It's eating me up inside. I can't handle it. I love her too much to keep this from her."

Shelby stepped closer to me and jammed her pointer finger toward my face. "You can't tell her. It will rip her to shreds."

I thought about Tamara's past. All the hurt and abuse she had already endured, and then being on the run for years, and now, what Shelby and I had done was going to be another blow to her already wounded heart. We would be one more story to add to the list of offenses done against her.

Why did I have to be this guy?

"Listen to me, Danny. We made a mistake. A stupid, drunken mistake that both of us will regret for the rest of our lives. It's never going to happen again."

"Never," I echoed her.

"Then why tell her? Don't you think it's better for us to suffer in our guilt than tell Tamara and break her heart? Not once but twice? Take the two people she cares about most away from her because *you* couldn't handle the guilt?"

I ran my hands through my hair and let out a breath. "I don't know …"

"You need to man up, Danny. You take that guilt that's eating at you, shove it down deep, lock it up, and throw away the flipping key."

I didn't know if I had the strength to do that. All the stuff with Marisa and my son had weakened my soul. I had been fighting two massive demons of guilt, and they both had been railing on me.

Shelby's phone rang. She backed away from me and dug

through her purse. Looking at the phone, she cursed under her breath before answering. From the expression on her face, it had to have been Tamara. "Hey, chica." She listened for a few minutes. "I'm sorry. Treasures? Yeah, I can meet you there." After a few more exchanges between her and Tamara, Shelby hung up.

Looking back up at me, all the anger had drained from her face. It was now replaced with sorrow. "We need to keep our secret for her, Danny." Tears gathered in her eyes, and her lower lip quivered. "Tamara has never told me much about her family or where she came from. But I've been around her enough to know that she's not involved in their lives. We're all she has. Don't take that from her."

Nothing in me wanted to take anything from her, ever, but we already had.

Tamara just didn't know it yet.

September 17, 4:00 p.m. – Tamara

It seemed asinine that Shelby would be the one I went to for advice about Danny. She hated him. But she was the only person I really trusted. I ordered us both a coffee and found a table outside, so I could smoke. I lit up and pulled out my phone.

`Got us coffee and a table outside.`

Taking in a drag, I looked around and considered how much I should tell Shelby. Would she hate Danny more, or have compassion on him if she knew the truth?

`Almost there.`

Pulling out my journal, I wrote as I waited for Shelby.

My heart is heavy. Why didn't I leave town before I fell so hard for Danny? A part of me wants to leave now, but I love him too much. I'm not ready to give up on him, but his excessive drinking has to stop! I understand running from pain but medicating it won't help. Medicating only leads to more pain, more reasons to medicate.

From the corner of my eye, I saw Shelby pull up in her '97

convertible Mustang with the top down. She blew me a kiss but didn't smile. Her normal bounce of energy wasn't there as she walked toward me. Was something bothering her, too? I hoped she could handle this conversation. Something had to change.

"Hey, chica." I slid my journal back into my purse, stood, and gave her a hug.

She held on tight for a long moment. "What's going on, sweet stuff?"

"It's Danny. I know you hate him, but I'm really worried about him."

She exhaled and took a seat. "Do you have another one of those smokes? I left mine in the car."

I tapped a cigarette out of the box and handed it to her. "Everything okay with you?"

"Yeah, things are fine." She lit up the cigarette and slowly inhaled. "What's going on with Danny?"

"Okay … but you seem kind of off." I took a sip of my coffee. I didn't want to be one of those people who were so consumed with their own problems that they missed it when their best friend was hurting.

"I'm good. A little hungover, but that's nothing new." She smiled, but it seemed forced. "Now, please tell me what's going on with you."

Leaning forward, I rested my head on my hand. *Do not get emotional.* I told her everything that Charlie had said to me the other night, when I'd been searching for Danny. Her emotions were hard to read as I shared the story.

When I was finished, Shelby sat back in her seat and brought her cigarette to her lips. Surely, she was preparing to go through the "I told you so" speech, and I completely deserved it.

"I think I may have rushed in way too quickly with him." I held my breath, already afraid of her response.

She sucked in a drag and blew out the smoke. "What do you want me to say?"

"I don't really know. Just say *something.* I have no idea what to do. He's drinking all the time, moping around like it's the end of the world. What she did to him was beyond messed up, but wallowing in it isn't helping. I wish things would go back to the way they were a week ago, when things were easy with us. But I don't know how to get back there, or if it's even possible." Tears pooled in my eyes. Why couldn't things actually work out well for once in my life? Was wanting love and a peaceful life too much to ask for?

"Are you thinking about leaving him?"

"No … I don't know … I don't think so, but I think he's already checked out of the relationship. It's like he's no longer interested or even capable of moving forward."

"Tamara, I'm not sure about many things, but I know Danny loves you." She smashed her cigarette into the ashtray. "More than you realize. You guys will get through this. Do you have another smoke?"

"Yeah, sure." I pulled out another and passed it to her. "So, you think I should stick it out? I thought you hated him. Where is this coming from?"

"I was wrong." She lit up again. "Danny is a good guy. Screwed up like the rest of us but good."

I sat back and cocked my head. "Are you serious right now? Have aliens abducted my best friend?"

"What's that supposed to mean?"

I had fully prepared myself for the Danny-hating Shelby I was used to. "Where is the girl who scoured the Internet, begged me not to move in with him, and assaulted him in the shower because you hated him?"

"I don't know what to tell you." She shrugged and flicked her ash onto the ground. "I see how good he is with you, and how he makes you feel. You seem genuinely happy when you are with him. If he makes you happy, he can't be that bad."

I gave her a skeptical smile. "Really, are you quoting Sheryl Crow to me?"

Shelby shrugged and gave a half-smile. "Well, she's brilliant."

"True." We both laughed. This is why I loved her so much. "So, you're okay with him now?"

"Yeah, I mean, you know my story, my dad abandoned me and my mom. So, the fact that Danny is so broken up about not being able to be there for his kid says a lot about his character. He's a good dad, even if he's not allowed to be, so that means he's a good man."

I nodded, taking in her words. It was strange that she was suddenly Team Danny after hating him so vehemently, but it was somewhat comforting to know that she was in my corner. Danny and I had built so much together already. I should give him my full support during this hard time.

I pulled out my phone to text Danny and noticed my half hour lunch break was almost over.

`Thinking about you. Love you.`

"I gotta go." I stood, leaned over, and gave her a big squeeze. "Thank you for meeting with me on a moment's notice. You're the best."

"Anything for my girl."

As I walked back to work, my phone dinged.

`Come straight home after work. I need to tell you something.`

September 17, 9:22 p.m. – Danny

My heart ached as I paced the living room, waiting for Tamara to return home from work. When I was younger, I believed there could be nothing more painful than what my mother did to me, but I was wrong. The most painful wounds in life are self-inflicted.

How was I ever going to find the strength to tell her what Shelby and I had done? Maybe I should tell her it was some random woman at the bar. That way, she would still have her best friend to turn to. But that felt dirty. Coming clean about everything was the right thing to do.

I sat on the couch, picked up my guitar, and finger-plucked a soft melody. Creating music had always been therapy for my soul. The last three days, I couldn't bring myself to play. Now, I needed something to give me strength.

The door handle turned, and Tamara walked through. Her shoulders sagged, and her eyes seemed tired. Everything in me wanted to go to her, wrap my arms around her, and forget all that had happened over the last couple of days.

I set my guitar in its case and patted the seat next to me. "Come sit."

She eyed me wearily and then slowly walked across the room.

My heart thudded against my ribcage, and my hands suddenly felt clammy. Moment of truth. Damn, this hurt. I'd already screwed up everything with Marisa and my son, and now, I was going to destroy the best thing that ever happened to me. Self-loathing turned my stomach, making me nauseous.

Tamara put her hand on my shoulder. "What's going on, Danny?"

I closed my eyes and took in a deep breath. "Do you ever wish you could go back in time and change the things you've done?"

She caressed my arm. The warmth of her touch felt like heaven. For a moment, I pretended this was all a bad dream.

"All the time," she finally said.

"Really?" Taken aback, my eyes opened.

"Absolutely. I have so many regrets, I can't begin to count them."

My gaze met hers. "But you seem so good."

"I'm not, though. You're always calling me your angel, but you don't know the things I've done."

"Oh, yeah?" Maybe there was hope. If she had made really big mistakes like I had, she might possibly find it in her heart to forgive me. Then we could move past all this and start over.

"This isn't about me right now, Danny. You said you had something to tell me."

I sucked in a sharp breath. "I do." I stood and walked to the fridge. "I could really use a beer. You want one?" Apprehension was burning a hole in my stomach. I needed something to calm the flame. I grabbed two beers out of the fridge.

"Danny, please. I've worried about you all day. You need to tell me." She still sat on the couch with a pleading expression on her face.

After setting the beers down on the counter, I knelt in front of her on the couch. "I'm sorry. I'm stalling. I just don't want you to hate me." I placed my hands on top of hers and brought them together as if I was saying a prayer. Mercy was the only thing that could save me now.

"I could never hate you." She looked at me with such love and adoration it hurt.

I didn't know if I could bear losing her. How could I make her understand? "Did I ever tell you how I started playing the guitar?"

She shook her head slightly as a line appeared between her brows.

I swallowed back the dread that had balled up in my throat. "I was eleven years old, and I had just discovered MTV. I was enthralled by the musicians, especially the guitarists as they played their riffs."

"I don't understand what this has to do with anything."

Unfortunately, she'd know soon enough. "I'm sorry. It's just part of the story." If she knew this part of me, maybe she'd understand.

Her mouth crooked up into a sad smile. "Okay. Please continue."

"For weeks, I begged my mom to let me take guitar lessons, but she was hesitant. She thought that if I wanted to learn music, it was best that I started with the piano, but I didn't want that. The guy on the keyboard wasn't the cool rock star I wanted to be." I hesitated for a moment. Tamara was the first person I had ever told this secret to.

"One day, after school, I left the house on my bike to meet some buddies at the park, but they never showed. When I got back to the house, Uncle Mike's car was parked in the driveway. He wasn't really my uncle, he was my dad's best friend. But I had always called him Uncle Mike."

I looked into Tamara's eyes to draw strength. Tamara worked one of her hands out from underneath mine and placed it on top of my hand, caressing it with tenderness.

"I heard strange noises coming from my parents' bedroom."

Tamara gasped, her face filling with horror.

"Messed up, right? I found them cheating on my dad."

"Danny, that's awful."

"She begged me not to tell my dad. She told me there were things I was too young to understand." All the emotion of that day flooded over me in a second. "She was lonely because my dad was at work all the time. It was so screwed up. My dad was out there, working long hours to support us, and she was screwing his best friend. The next day, she enrolled me in guitar lessons." A thick lump formed in my throat, making it hard to speak. "I hated her for it, but I kept her secret. You're the first person I've ever told."

She leaned down and put her hand on my face. Compassion filled her eyes. "Thank you for trusting me enough to share."

Closing my eyes, I savored the comfort of her touch. Though I didn't deserve it, I needed to pretend for a few more moments. I forced my eyes open and locked my gaze on her. "I promised myself I'd never be like her. But the truth is… I *became* her."

Fear flitted across her face, and she pulled her hand away. "What are you saying?"

Panic jolted through my core. I couldn't be the one who hurt her like this. Perhaps my mother was right all those years ago. Telling the truth would cause more pain than it was worth. Shelby's words echoed in my head. *Shove it down deep, lock it up, and throw away the flipping key.* But telling her the truth about Marisa could at least explain some of my strange behavior. Maybe that was enough, for now. I could confess who I was, without completely destroying the woman I loved.

"I'm talking about with Marisa. There's something I need

to tell you. I know I've been distant for the last few days. And I know you know why. This stuff with Marisa and my son, it's killing me."

Relief washed over her lovely features. She knelt down on the floor with me, coming down to my level. "Whatever it is, you can tell me. I'm not going anywhere."

I swallowed hard. "When I told you I cheated on Marisa the last night we were together, it wasn't true."

Her eyebrows furrowed. "What do you mean?"

"Did I tell you Marisa was the first woman I'd ever been with?" A vein pulsed in my neck.

She shook her head.

"She was. And I swear I loved her, but she was all I really knew."

Man, this was almost as hard as telling her the truth about Shelby. She might still want to walk away. And that's what she should have done.

"I only told you half the truth that night on the beach." Tears gathered in my eyes. I hated what I'd done to Marisa. And I hated what I'd done to Tamara. "Things were good with us, but when I turned twenty-three, things changed. I had been booking gigs at local bars, and women were throwing themselves at me all the time. I was young and so, so dumb. Truth is, I gave in to the temptation—not just once but many times. By the time she found out, I had been cheating on her for a while." Sorrow consumed every part of me.

There seemed to be conflicting emotions happening inside Tamara. She was still on the floor with me, but her body was rigid, and her face was hard to read.

"I hurt her, Tamara. And now, she's doing everything she can to hurt me. I'm getting exactly what I deserve." Tears slid down my cheeks.

Tamara was silent for a long while. Every breath felt like it took a thousand years. Would she be able to forgive me for lying to her? Would she want to stay with someone like me? I wished for both. I wanted her to stay and save me from myself. I wanted her to leave me and save herself.

Finally, she took hold of my hand and spoke. "Nobody deserves what she's doing to you. You've made big mistakes. We all have. But to deprive your son of such a good dad is plain wrong." She kissed my cheek where the tears were falling.

I slid my arms around her. "How can you say that I'm a good dad?"

She pulled back, her eyes searching mine. "If you were in his life, you'd teach him the guitar and how to write songs. And though you'd discipline him, you'd never abuse him. You'd be a great father."

"How do you know?" I whispered, my voice cracking.

"Because I know your heart." Her words stung because I knew the truth. I was a man who hadn't learned his lesson, a man who had cheated on this beautiful soul with her best friend. But I would change. I drew her close again. She was the most wonderful thing that had ever happened to me. That she knew some of the worst things about me and still believed in me was more than I could ever ask or imagine was possible.

"You think so?"

"I *know* so, Danny. I've never had a guy treat me as well as you do."

I ran my fingers through her hair and rested my forehead on hers. "How can you see the good in me after everything I just told you?"

"I put on my rose-colored glasses right before I came home."

I laughed and kissed her slowly and sweetly. "No. It's because you're my angel." I stood, pulled her to her feet, picked her up, and carried her to our bedroom.

Somehow, some way, I would find a way to make up for my mistake.

September 18, 4:12 p.m. – Tamara

`I'm going to be home a little later than expected.`

I hit send and ran to my car, water from the puddles splashing my feet. I wasn't supposed to work today, but when they called first thing this morning and asked me to cover a mid-morning shift, I jumped on the opportunity. Though I had been calm and sweet to Danny last night after his confession, I woke up to a horrible dream that he had cheated on me. It left me feeling hollow and angry. If he was able to cheat on Marisa over and over again while claiming to love her, who was to say he wouldn't do the same to me? And if he was able to keep the cheating from her, what's to say he would even tell me if he did.

I slammed the door to my car closed and pulled out of the parking lot. I had been wrestling with my thoughts all through my shift. They were consuming me and I had to talk to someone.

There was no way I could tell Shelby. Finding out he cheated multiple times on his pregnant girlfriend would completely change her tune about him, and if I decided to stay, I needed her in my corner. The only other person that I trusted in Ocean Shores was Charlie. A light sprinkling of rain covered my windshield as I drove toward Midway's.

There were only two cars in the parking lot, and Charlie's was one of them. Things wouldn't get busy for another hour or so. This conversation wouldn't take that long. Not that I even had a clue as to what I was going to say. All I knew was that I needed a sounding board who was already privy to Danny's story. Turning off my car, I leaned over the steering wheel, head throbbing from a depression headache. My phone pinged.

How much later?

I sucked in a large breath. I wasn't sure. A part of me didn't want to go home at all. Maybe I could crash at Shelby's tonight and sort out the crap that was going through my head. But then she would want details, and I couldn't go there.

An hour or so...

I exited my car and shoved my phone into my back pocket as I ran for the bar.

An old man sat at the counter, hunched over a dark beer. Charlie stood behind the bar, drying glasses and putting them away. He looked up and gave me his wide grin.

I tried to smile back, but the muscles in my face wouldn't yield to my brain's command.

"Hey, Tam, what can I get for you?" Confusion settled over his face, and he peered around me. "Where's Danny?"

I averted my eyes. Was Charlie really the right person to talk to about this?

"Is everything all right?" Charlie said after an awkward moment of silence.

I glanced at the gentleman at the counter before making eye contact again. "I'm not sure. Do you have a few minutes?"

"I always have time for you. Can I get you a drink or something?"

I shook my head. "I was hoping we could talk in private."

He put down the glass he was drying. "Yeah, okay." Turning to the customer, he said, "Hey, Rich, you good for now? I'm going to take a short break."

Rich lifted his half-empty beer. "Maybe you should pour me another before you go, just in case."

Charlie nodded, filled an icy mug, and then followed me out the back door. The rain had stopped, but the air was still moist, and gray clouds loomed on the horizon. Charlie pulled out a pack of smokes. "You want one?"

"Sure."

He handed me a cigarette and lit it for me before lighting his own. "What's going on?"

I took a long drag of the smoke. "Well … Danny dropped a big one on me last night."

"Oh, yeah? What did he say?" Charlie averted his gaze, almost as if he expected what I was about to say.

"He told me that he hadn't just cheated on Marisa one time while they were separated, that it happened many times."

Charlie nodded, his gaze still plastered to the ground. Obviously, this wasn't new knowledge to him. The smoke from his cigarette swirled upward, disappearing into the wind. He fidgeted with his lighter, then kicked at a pebble next to his foot.

The atmosphere around us felt thick with tension.

Charlie took in a deep breath and looked up at me, his soft gaze locking with mine. "Tamara, this may be out of line, but I've wanted to say this for a long time. Danny … he's not good for you." He paused for a moment, seeming to struggle with his words. "You shouldn't stay with him."

His words smacked me in the gut and anger immediately rose in me. "Seriously, Charlie, why are you saying this now, after so many months, knowing I was falling for him?"

"I wanted so badly to." He tapped his cigarette, flicking off the ash. "I tried to drop hints, but it didn't feel like it was my place to tell you what you should do with your life."

"So, you let me fall in love with a freaking cheater?" I pounded my cigarette into the side of the Dumpster and let it drop to the ground.

"Tamara, I—"

"No. Just stop talking." I raised my hands in exasperation. "I actually thought you were my friend, but to keep this kind of information from me because you didn't feel it was your place is just—" My mind fumbled for the right word. "—cowardly, Charlie. You had plenty of chances to do more than *hint* that the man I was falling in love with had sex with other women multiple times while he was with his pregnant girlfriend. No decent, self-respecting man would ever keep that from a friend."

Charlie's face twisted in pain. "That's so not fair. You seemed to have plenty of information when we talked at the bar that day. Don't blame me for stepping into your relationship with Danny, eyes wide shut. And just so you know, I told him to stay away from you. That you were way too good for him. But honestly, I felt wrong interfering in any way." He took in a large breath his expression softening. "The fact is, Tamara, I've had feelings for you for a long time. I didn't want to be led by selfish motives."

"What?" I blinked rapidly.

"You heard me." He took a step closer.

His honesty unhinged me. All the anger drained away, and I could feel tears threatening to come. "I'm sorry, Charlie. What I said was unfair. I'm just so angry at the situation. Truth is, I was gearing up to leave town before things happened with Danny."

"Maybe you should leave town now."

"It's not that easy." There were nightmares he didn't know about that had been chasing me for years. Then Danny had come along and swept me off my feet and promised me he'd keep me safe. But Danny had his own problems, his own skeletons in the closet. The kind that wouldn't just hurt my body but destroy my soul as well. I didn't know if I could survive if Danny broke my heart like that. I looked down at my feet as the tears spilled over. "I have the money to leave now. I just don't know if I have the strength."

"You should give yourself more credit. In my line of work, I get to know people. Most of the time, I'm an excellent judge of character. From the moment I met you, I knew you were strong. Not only that, but you're good. I see the way you're such a true friend to Shelby. Even when she's being selfish, you let her have her way. I *see* you, Tamara. If you want to stand on your own, you can."

"That's it? I should just leave town? After everything you just said, I would think you would want me to stick around."

Charlie tilted his head. "I *do* want you here but more than that, I want what's best for you. Ocean Shores is beneath you and getting away from Danny and Shelby would be best. Maybe there's more for you somewhere else, like a bigger city. Us small towners are holding you back." Charlie gave me a sad smile.

I wiped away the tears that had been falling down my face. "Before Danny, I was planning to leave Washington altogether. This is where all the bad stuff happened. But I don't know ..."

"Just pray about it." The corner of his mouth lifted.

"You really *are* getting religious, aren't you?"

He chuckled. "Naw, I just think everyone needs a bit of divine help every once in a while."

"We'll see." I stepped toward him and then wrapped my arms around his broad shoulders. "Thank you, Charlie. You are a good friend. Sorry again for what I said earlier."

He gave me a tight squeeze. "You take care of yourself, girl."

On the way back to my car, Danny's confession hit me again, along with the dream and the pain it carried. Pounding the steering wheel, I swore again and again. Why did Danny have to lie to me? Why did I have to love him so much? Something in me wanted to run away and never look back. To shut him out like I'd done to everyone and everything else, but even the thought of it stole the breath from my lungs.

I pulled the car into Danny's driveway and slammed the gear into park. Yes, it was wrong of him to withhold the truth from me, but in some way, I understood why he'd done it. Since he was a little boy, he had been taught that lying kept the ones he loved safe. Until four days ago, there were never any doubts that he loved me. Now, that was all I felt. Doubt mixed with anger and regret.

I stared at Danny's house. The one that was supposed to be my safe place. Now, it looked like a dungeon, filled with so many raw emotions to haunt me. I couldn't face Danny like this. I shut the car off, grabbed my jacket on the way out, and walked toward the beach.

Donning my coat, I took in the massive waves crashing against the shore. Gusts of wind flew across my face, causing my dark hair to whip around me. The ocean spray pelted my face, and the sting of it almost felt good—a welcome reprieve from the turmoil in my heart. But the thoughts that assaulted me were louder than the windstorm that was brewing.

Why hadn't I just left town before Danny? Sticking to my plan would have been the safest bet for me. I cursed into the wind. I was so stupid for buying into the fantasy that Danny could protect me, that he would never hurt me, that I could be safe with him. To find out he'd been lying to me this whole time was too much to just forgive and forget, right?

Another large gust of wind blew around me, and I screamed into it. I was such an idiot for letting myself become dependent on a guy, especially a guy like Danny. This whole time, I thought his love was saving me. What a naïve little girl I was. Danny wasn't this perfect, protective Superman of my dreams. He was just a different kind of abuser set in my path to hurt me. An abuser of trust. I kicked the sand as the brutal wind blew across the coastal shore.

Why had I let my heart lead me into this trap? I wanted to run away from all this confusion, but I also wanted to stay and be loved. How could I possibly make this decision? Just then, Charlie's words hit me colder than the ocean winds. *Just pray about it.* I clenched my fists.

Did Charlie actually believe there was this all-powerful being who would tell me what to do?

Wouldn't that be nice? My prayers had never worked before. Why should I pray now? God was the one who had put me in this situation in the first place.

Turning toward Danny's house, my heart broke a little more. His house had become my home. The only home I had for over three and a half years. The lights were on and a sense of warmth seemed to emanate from it. It was the most beautiful, love-filled home I had ever experienced. Was I ready to give that up because there was a possibility that Danny would cheat on me in the future?

My heart softened as I thought of our last couple of months together. He'd been nothing but sweet and kind since we met. Yes, he'd lied to me, but everything else had been amazing. Too wonderful to give up. It was unfair to judge him for things he'd done before we got together. Marisa had already punished him enough for his past sins. With all he'd lost, surely, he'd learned his lesson. Danny was a broken and wounded man, but he was the man I loved.

I pulled out my phone to message him and apologize for not coming right in. When I opened my phone, I saw he'd already messaged me.

`Come in when you're ready, angel. I made you something.`

His words struck that raw chord in me—the one that desperately wanted to be loved. As I approached the house, a familiar smell wafted around me. I opened the door to see Danny standing behind the kitchen island. He looked up, his eyes warm and adoring.

For the first time that day, I felt hope rise in me. "What's this?" I walked across the room, rested my hands on the island and looked around. Two candles were lit on the island and a bottle of champagne sat chilling in an ice bucket next to the stove.

"Love dumplings." He moved the tray over to the island. "But this time, I managed to not burn them."

I smiled at the memory of our first date. Water dripped from my hair onto the floor. I must have looked like a drowned rat.

Danny's eyes landed on me and heat spread through my core. He still had a way of making me go weak in the knees with a single look. He walked around the counter and helped me out of my jacket. Pulling aside my wet hair, he kissed my neck and whispered in my ear, "I'm so sorry, my sweet angel."

My heart turned into mush. I turned around and put my arms around his neck. "All is forgiven." I brought my lips to his.

He kissed me back deeply, in this meaningful way, his lips communicating how sorry he truly was. He pulled back after a while, his head resting against mine. "I was hoping tonight would be a new beginning for us. That we could let all that old stuff go and just start over."

"Not a chance," I said

His face fell. "Okay."

"Danny, I've loved almost every moment we've shared together. I don't want to start over. I want to pick up where we left off four days ago."

A huge smile broke across his face. "I'll take it."

November 19, 10:30 a.m. – Tamara

"Happy birthday!" I kissed Danny's cheek while holding a bowl of waffle mix. Waffles weren't the best birthday breakfast, but it was one of his favorites. And one that I could actually cook.

He smiled back. "Thanks. Anything I can do to help?"

"You can grab the fixings while I grill these bad boys up." I placed the bowl on the island and pulled out the waffle maker.

"Sure thing." Danny went to the fridge and pulled out the strawberries and chocolate while whistling the tune to "What a Wonderful World."

"Where is the whipped cream?"

I walked over and inspected the fridge, searching for the missing item. "Shoot. I must have forgotten it. I'm sorry, babe."

"No worries. It's a beautiful morning. I'll take a stroll down to the store."

I wrapped my arms around his neck and planted a kiss on his soft lips. "Thank you. I'll have everything else ready when you get back."

"Deal." Danny grinned and kissed me again before heading out the door.

It was good to have the Danny I loved back. Two months had passed since he confessed his secrets. The depression had gradually lifted from him. He quit drinking heavily and came back to his normal self. Those first few weeks, there still seemed to be a bit of a wall between us, but I couldn't tell if it was because of my own suspicions and hurt, or because of something that was on the inside of him. The walls eventually crumbled, though, and I let my defenses down. Somewhere over the last few months, I fell even harder for him.

I dumped some of the mix into the waffle maker and ran into the bedroom to grab my savings. I broke open my wine jar and counted. A little under two grand. I shoved the wad of cash into a Crown Royal bag and buried it in the bottom of my purse. Today, I would trade my savings for his birthday gift, and it warmed my heart. If I did this, it meant I was all-in. No more running in fear.

I thought about Ryan for a minute, something I hadn't done in months. When I moved in with Danny, the nightmares had stopped, and I wasn't sure why. Had something changed? I thought about it for a while and then picked up my phone. I opened the Google search engine, heart racing. If I typed in his name, could he somehow track me? The waffle iron dinged. The first round of waffles were done. I set my phone aside, took the waffles out and poured in some batter before reaching for my phone once more. I typed Ryan's full name into the search engine.

Several links down, an article popped out at me. The headline read, "*Small Town Raid Leads to a Major Drug Bust.*"

The words touched my soul like a kiss from heaven itself. The date beside the article said it was over four months old. Not long after Danny and I moved in together. Could it be that my luck was finally changing? I clicked on the link and read about how Ryan's house had been raided because of an anonymous tip. They found over an ounce of meth, along with scales. That made it a class-B felony, and, if convicted, he could serve up to ten years in prison.

Relief flooded into every part of my being. This was the big break I'd been waiting for. I didn't have to run anymore. With tears of joy in my eyes, I took the waffle out of the maker and put it on Danny's plate. I plopped a bit more batter into the maker and started cutting the strawberries. I began to fantasize about Danny and I spending the rest of our lives here in this quaint town, raising our own babies and giving them the loved we shared. With the upbringing I had, and after years of being on the run, I never thought I'd have a normal life.

When Danny returned, I handed him the plate of the waffles and completed it with the chocolate, strawberries, and almost the whole container of whipped cream. As we ate and talked, I wanted to tell him about Ryan, but bringing up my ex-boyfriend on his birthday felt wrong. Instead, we talked about our plans for the day, and my heart sunk. He had wanted to spend the day with me, but I had gotten the call the night before from Yenney's Music Store in Grays Harbor that the twelve-string guitar I special-ordered for him was finally in, and I had to drive to the other side of the bay to pick it up.

"Oh, I'm sorry. I got called into work today while you were gone." It bothered me to lie, and I was a terrible liar, but I believed he bought it.

"Can't you call in sick?" He stood and cleared the table.

"That's the problem. You know, I wasn't scheduled. But two of the waitresses came down with the flu." I hated leaving him on his birthday, but after tonight, it would be worth it. I couldn't wait to see the look on his face when I gave the guitar to him.

Danny set our plates in the sink. He walked back to the table, stood behind me, and massaged my shoulders. "But I had plans for us today."

Chills swept through me at his touch.

Leaning over, his lips caressed my shoulder and made a trail up my neck. "And most of those plans involved keeping you locked up in the bedroom."

A moan escaped my lips. "I have a few minutes before I have to leave."

He pulled me to my feet and led me to the bedroom.

Being tangled up in Danny's arms after making love made it even harder to leave.

"I love you, Tamara." he whispered as his fingers caressed my arms. "I didn't think this kind of happiness was possible for me. Not after everything."

My heart expanded. "Me neither."

"Promise me you'll never leave me." His voice was a bit hoarse.

I lifted my head off his chest. "Never, Danny. I promise." I thought about the money in the bottom of my purse. It was once intended for an escape fund. Now, it would be used to give him that beautiful twelve-string guitar I'd seen him drooling over on the Internet. Because I didn't need to escape anymore. Danny was my ultimate escape.

November 19, 9:45 p.m. – Danny

Twenty-five years old. For some reason, that number felt heavy. A quarter-century. Shouldn't I have accomplished more than playing at an occasional open mic night at my cousin's bar by now? Ignoring the chatter of our friends, I stared into the bonfire, pondering those deep questions. Tamara sat next to me on a lawn chair, her head resting on my arm. She had set up this party on our patio, facing the beach, after she had worked half the day. It was a typical cold and windy November night in Ocean Shores. At least it wasn't raining, and I had Tamara to keep me warm. It was nice to have some of my friends over, but part of me wished it was only me and her.

Tamara had come home earlier than I had expected, which was a nice surprise. She came loaded up with a case of Coors and a fifth of Crown Royal and told me our friends would be here soon. We had shared a few beers before everyone showed up. As soon as Charlie, Milly, Caiden, and Shelby had arrived, they began egging each other on to take shots.

It was hard to be around Shelby. Being this close to her was a horrible reminder of what I had done a couple of months ago. More than once, she had almost cost me my relationship with Tamara. I couldn't hate her, though. In some ways, I pitied her. Just like I pitied myself. She's the one I should have ended up with because she was pretty close to a female version of myself. The reason she clung to Tamara so hard was the same reason I did. Tamara was her light. And us bugs were always attracted to the light. We needed it in order to survive. In all fairness, I should've pitied Tamara, too. But I adored her too much for that.

"Hey, chica, do another shot with me," Shelby said.

Tamara snuggled tighter against my arm. "I don't know, girl. I have to work tomorrow."

"You just can't handle your liquor." Shelby wiggled her eyebrows.

"Oooh, that sounds like a challenge," Caiden piped in.

"I say it's time for *everyone* to do a shot." Charlie stood and grabbed the bottle of Crown.

"I like the way you think, Charlie." Shelby lifted her cup for him to fill it.

Leaning over, I squeezed Tamara's hand. "You don't have to if you don't want to."

She looked up at me and smiled. "It's fine. I want to celebrate with you. Believe me, I can hold my own with Shelby."

"I know you can, angel." I kissed her and then leaned back.

Charlie made the rounds with the whiskey, free-pouring shots into everyone's Solo cups.

"Three, two, one, shoot!" Charlie yelled and everyone tipped their cups back. The shot burned on the way down, and my vision blurred a bit as the fire danced along the backdrop of the ocean.

"Well, that did the bottle in." Charlie turned the bottle upside down, but nothing came out.

"It's cool, man," I said. "We have some more beer in the house."

"Isn't it about time for gifts?" Shelby's voice had a hint of mischief in it.

Tamara stood, with renewed pep in her demeanor. "Actually, yes. I think it's the *perfect* time for gifts."

"You guys didn't need to get me anything."

"Yeah, we did, old man." Shelby laughed. "Twenty-five is kind of a big number."

I glared at her. "You're so funny, I forgot to laugh."

She stuck out her tongue, reached into her purse, and pulled out a gift. Based on the poor wrapping job, it was obviously a bottle. And knowing Shelby, it was definitely alcohol. She handed it to me.

"I'll be right back," Tamara said.

"Don't you want to see what I got him?" Shelby turned to her.

"That's okay. I'm pretty sure I know what's inside." Tamara opened the sliding glass door. "Alcohol!" She called over her shoulder.

"Tamara!" Shelby shouted after her.

I ripped off the wrapping paper and turned over the bottle of darkened liquid.

It wasn't …

Lagavulin Islay Single Malt Scotch Whisky aged 16 years. My jaw dropped. "You bought me a bottle of Lagavulin 16?"

"It *is* still your favorite drink, isn't it?"

"Yes, it is, but this is expensive."

"Then let's not let it go to waste." She lifted her cup in the air. "Pop that baby open and let's have another shot."

I rolled my eyes and threw the crumpled wrapping paper into the fire. "You don't shoot Lagavulin, Shelby."

"You do when I buy it for you." She put a hand on her hip. "Besides, you sound like a little wuss when you say things like that."

"I'll drink to that." Caiden laughed.

"All right, but it feels a bit sacrilegious." I lifted the bottle in the air. "Charlie, would you like to pour for us again?"

"Hey, man, just because I'm a bartender doesn't mean I love to pour alcohol. It's your birthday. You do the honors."

I opened up the bottle and the smoky-sweet scent filled my nostrils. Man, I loved this stuff. That was actually a really thoughtful gift from Shelby. Way more than I would have expected from her. I stood and walked around to each person, filling all their cups.

"Hey, Shelby, where's Nick tonight?" Milly said.

That was a good question. I figured he'd be here after he got off work.

"Let's just say he won't be joining us this evening. Or ever, if I have anything to say about it."

They had broken up? Interesting.

Shelby picked up her shot. "Three, two, one. Shoot."

I downed the Lagavulin. It burned so well on the way down. Tamara's hand gently touched my shoulder.

She was next to me again with a guitar case in her hands.

"Chica," Shelby said, "you just missed the best shot in the world. Come here and I'll pour you one."

"I'm good. Thanks, though."

"This is your man's twenty-fifth birthday." Shelby pointed at me. "That means we need to do at least twenty-five shots tonight. That's four per person."

What was Shelby thinking, egging Tamara on like that? "Come on, Shelby," I said. "I think we already passed that quota an hour ago without Tamara's help." Just because she was hurting didn't mean she needed to bring Tamara down with her.

"I just wanted to give Danny his gift." Tamara set the guitar case in front of me.

There was a big red bow on top.

"Wow, angel, this case is awesome."

She shook her head and pushed the case toward me. "Open

it."

I took it from her, unfastened the latches, and lifted the lid. Inside was the Martin Grand Performance twelve-string guitar I'd wanted for years. A large lump formed in the back of my throat. I'd never had someone do something so special for me. "This is an eighteen-hundred-dollar guitar. Where did you get this kind of money?"

"I had a little stashed away."

Across from me, Shelby's eyes grew wide as her mouth dropped open. A pang of guilt the size of Mount Rushmore tore through my guts. Who was this beautiful angel woman that stood in front of me? No matter how hard I tried, I'd never be good enough for her.

"You used your savings on this?" I took in the magnificent instrument, running my hand down the galvanized wood. I'd wanted this guitar for years. But it felt so wrong that she'd spent most, if not all, of her savings on me—the ultimate liar and cheat. "I don't know what to say."

"How about you just play me a song before I head to bed?"

"Absolutely," I said, overwhelmed. My shaking fingers found the G-chord, and I ran my other hand across the strings. The sound was stunning. Better than I'd even imagined. They must have tuned it for her at the music store. I started to finger-pluck the tune of the song I'd written for her months ago.

"I was born in an American town
where the mountains touch the face of God
and she was born on the wrong side of the tracks."

I looked up at her. She stood before me, hands folded in front of her face as if she was saying a prayer. In the moonlight, tears glistened on her cheeks. She gazed at me as if I had hung the sun, the moon, and the stars. As if she believed in me. As if I was capable of doing everything my heart had ever dreamed of.

All I could think about was how big of a liar I was. She thought I was some sort of hero. Really, I was a fraud. A lying sack of crap that didn't deserve a bit of her love. And yet, she *did* love me, but as I sang, I struggled to feel worthy.

"One night, she came into my arms.
She said, I've been through hell, but you can take what's left.
What's left of that girl is a fallen angel. What's left is a fallen angel.
What's left is a chance of a new life in the arms of this cowboy.
What's left is a will to carry on when you thought your life was over.
What's left is a fallen angel for me, just for me."

The first time I'd sung her that song, it felt like a promise. Now, it felt like a lie. A lie with enough weight to drag my soul to hell. I finished the song, and everyone clapped.

"Outstanding song, Danny," Charlie said. "You've gotten way better."

"I have a wonderful muse." I kept my eyes on Tamara.

Milly sighed dramatically. "I wish a guy would write songs like that about me."

"You're making the rest of mankind look bad, McMillan," Caiden said, with a chuckle.

I placed the guitar in the case, stood, and put my arms around Tamara. "I love you," I whispered in her ear. I held her tight for a long moment, wishing the dreadful feelings of guilt would quit bludgeoning my insides. I'd been really happy with Tamara these last few months. I'd done exactly what Shelby had told me to do. I'd shoved down the guilt and locked it up. But somehow, this extravagant gift she'd just given me was the key that smashed the door open. "Do you want me to go in with you?"

"No, you stay and have fun with our friends. Happy Birthday, Danny. I love you." She kissed me and walked into the house and closed the door behind her.

November 19, 11:56 p.m. – Danny

Two hours later, the bottle of Lagavulin had a sizable dent in it, but the guilt in my guts hadn't lessened at all. Caiden and Milly had left about a half hour ago, which left Charlie and Shelby. Shelby and I had drank most of the scotch.

"Hey, you guys. What do you think about turning this party up a notch?" Shelby said, her eyebrows moving up and down.

"This party seems to be about over, party girl," Charlie said.

Shelby reached into her purse. "What if I told you I scored some OxyContin earlier today?" She held up a small plastic bag.

"I don't know, Shelby," I said, though a big part of me wanted to. Taking an Oxy was sure to provide some momentary relief from the guilt demons tormenting my soul. "Tamara has always been pretty against drugs. It wouldn't be good if she found out."

"I second that." Charlie nodded.

"Oh, come on, Danny. It's your birthday," she purred, her voice velvety and seductive. "Let loose a little. If Tamara finds out, I'll take the fall for it."

"You promise?"

She nodded slowly, with a suggestive smile.

I stuck out my hand.

"Seriously, Danny? You're going to let her egg you on like

that?" Charlie said, his voice gruff.

"Yep." Getting high and forgetting seemed like the perfect birthday present to myself.

Shelby dropped the little pill in my hand.

I popped it in my mouth and washed it down with a sip of scotch.

Shelby took one too.

Charlie stood, the expression on his face indignant. "I don't want any part of this."

"You're such a stick-in-the-mud." Shelby glared up at him.

"I'd rather be a stick-in-the-mud than a horrible person."

Shelby leapt out of her seat and slapped Charlie across the face. "Don't you dare talk to me like that!" She hit his arm and pounded his chest.

"Hey!" I jumped out of my chair and pulled Shelby away from him. "Calm down. You're going to wake up Tamara."

Charlie's gaze bounced back and forth between our faces, his features lined with disgust. "You're just as bad as she is, Danny. Tamara deserves so much better than you both."

Anger welled up inside of me. I lunged forward, hands curling into fists. "Get out of here, before I do something I regret."

"Because I care about Tamara and don't want to interrupt her sleep tonight, I'm going to pretend like you didn't just threaten me."

Adrenaline pulsed through me as I watched Charlie storm out of the yard. Everything in me wanted to run after him and beat the arrogance out of him. I paced back and forth a few times before looking over at Shelby.

She picked up her purse and pulled out her pack of smokes. "That was a real buzzkill," she said.

"Are you all right?"

Her face had gone ashen. "I will be after a smoke and

another shot." She tapped out a cigarette and dug for a lighter.

I laughed a humorless laugh, grabbed the scotch, took a large swig from the bottle, and handed it to her. "You have another smoke? I'm out."

"I'm running low, but I'll share." She handed me her smoke and then tipped back the bottle.

I wasn't sure if it was the adrenaline, the pill kicking in, or the last shot, but I started to feel strangely euphoric. I took a drag of the smoke and handed it back to Shelby.

Shelby set the bottle on the chair next to her and began to cry. She had always had such a fun party girl exterior. Something about the sight of her suddenly broken unhinged me.

"I thought you only needed a shot?" I said, trying to lighten the moment.

Her cries became more intense. I wanted to cry, too. All night, I had needed some sort of emotional release. The usual self-medicating wasn't working. I pulled her into my arms. "Just forget about him, Shelby. He just needs to get knocked off his gigantic high horse."

"He's right, though. I *am* a horrible person. No man will ever really love me," she said through sobs, crying into my shoulder. "My own father didn't even love me. How can any other man?"

"What about Nick? He seemed like he was really into you."

She lifted her head, eyes glistening and intense. "He never once looked at me the way you look at Tamara. He only ever loved my body. Just like every other man in my life." She turned her head away from my gaze. "That was true of my dad as well." Her voice was barely audible, but her words hit my heart like she'd screamed them through a megaphone. Had her dad touched her? Everything about her shifted in my mind. She wasn't a horrible person. She was a *broken* person. Always trying to keep the pain at bay. And I was just like all the other men in her life. I had used her for her body.

"I'm so sorry, Shelby."

Lifting her head, her gaze met mine. There was something in her eyes that was impossible to understand.

"Do you want to know what's horrible?" She paused, seeming to fight an inner battle. "I think about you sometimes."

Heat filled my stomach and pulsed slowly through my body. I tried never to think about her, but sometimes, I did. They were never pure thoughts.

"And when you were singing that song to Tamara, for a moment, I closed my eyes and pretended you were singing to me." Her lips inched closer to mine.

This was so wrong. I knew I should run in the opposite direction, to make her stop talking, but I couldn't move. I was hypnotized by the thrumming spike of adrenaline that was swirling through my veins, pulling me to her.

"Do you ever live in a fantasy world? Where you get everything you ever wanted?" Her lips barely touched mine, and I was a man on fire.

Stop this. I had to stop this.

She slid her hand around my shoulders, then up through my hair, pushing herself into me.

Desire pulsed through me, fueled by the pills and the booze. There was no stopping this tidal wave. No stopping this passion that raged between us. The only thing that mattered was the way her lips caused my body to ignite into something wild. Feral.

"We need to get out of here," Shelby whispered and pulled me forward. We staggered out of the gate and into the back of her car, where we once again sacrificed our souls to the darkness.

December 8, 7:53 p.m. – Tamara

Instead of going home after work, I decided to get a drink at Midway's. I texted Shelby to see if she wanted to join, but she said she wasn't up to coming out. A strange response, coming from Shelby. She was usually the one trying to get me to go out with her, but I hadn't seen her much in the two-and-a-half weeks since Danny's birthday. I lit a cigarette, started my car, and tried not to worry.

Ever since Danny's birthday, the wall had returned between us, and I was clueless as to why. The morning after the party, I'd found him passed out on the couch. Cleaning up after the party outside, I realized why he hadn't come to bed. He probably couldn't make it that far with all the alcohol he had consumed. Both fifths were emptied, and so was the case of beer.

Over the next few days, he moped around, seeming to nurse his hangover, but over two weeks had passed since then, and his depression never lifted. It was beginning to scare me. I'd heard that musicians could be moody, but this was borderline ludicrous. What made me even sadder was that I hadn't once seen him pick up the guitar I'd bought him since the night I gave it to him. Pulling into Midway's, I took a final drag off my smoke and smashed it into the ashtray. I exited the car and walked into the bar, digging out my fake ID. In less than a month, it would be obsolete.

The bar was fairly slow. Just a few patrons playing pool and a couple sitting at the bar.

"This place is dead," I said to Charlie as I took a seat on the stool.

"Hey, Tamara." He eyed me warily. Definitely not his normal, overly-friendly self. "Is Danny with you?"

His words hit me in a strange way. Danny was *always* with me. "Nope. Flying solo tonight."

"Hmm. No Shelby either?"

I shook my head. "Can I get a Long Island?"

His eyebrows pinched together, and a line appeared between them. "Is everything all right?"

"I will be after you get me that drink and stop asking so many questions," I said, with more attitude than I meant to.

He raised his hands. "Yes, ma'am. Long Island Iced Tea, coming right up." He filled a shaker with ice and poured in vodka, tequila, rum, and triple sec. He added sweet and sour, then shook it up and poured it into a hurricane glass before setting it in front of me.

"Thanks," I said and took a large gulp.

Charlie gave me the same wary look as he had before.

I glanced around the bar and leaned toward him. "What do you know?"

"About?" The line between Charlie's eyebrows became deeper.

"Come on, Charlie. You're acting weird. You usually at least smile at me when I come in, but you keep looking at me like something bad has happened."

He took in a deep breath. "I'm not the only one acting weird."

I stirred my drink with the straw. "How do you figure?"

He raised his hand and put out his pointer finger. "Well, number one, you're here by yourself. That never happens. And two." He stuck out his middle finger. "You never drink anything harder than beer unless Shelby is egging you on."

He had a point. Danny's depression had gotten to me. I took another large swallow of the iced tea and leaned back in the stool. "I don't know how to explain it. Things have just been really strained with Danny and me since his birthday party. It's like he's hiding behind some invisible barrier, and I can't bust through."

Something dark crept over Charlie's face, and he averted his gaze. "I need to go check on my customers."

Angst made a ball in the pit of my stomach. He knew something and, again, he was refusing to tell me. I finished my tea in one final, large gulp, and set down the empty glass.

At the other end of the bar, Charlie was laughing at something one of the guys said.

I shot daggers at him with my eyes. How could he be laughing at a time like this?

He stayed down there for a while, avoiding my looks.

"Charlie, can I get a refill?" I finally said, my tone sharp.

Face solemn, he walked toward me. He went through the same routine as before and placed the fresh drink in front of me. "You're not driving, are you?"

"I was. But I can walk home if I need to."

"It's freezing out there."

"You say that like you care." I cursed him under my breath.

His expression became soft. "You *know* I care, Tamara. Way more than you could imagine."

"Then tell me what you know," I demanded.

He shook his head. "I don't want to cause problems."

"My boyfriend is a freaking zombie and has been since his birthday, so why don't you cut the crap and tell me what happened?"

"If I tell you, you can't say a word."

"My lips are sealed." My gaze bore into his. I wasn't leaving without answers.

Doubt lined his features. "You promise?"

"You know I'm trustworthy, Charlie, so spill it."

He looked around the room and leaned in real close. "Shelby brought drugs to the party."

Drugs? A wound I had buried deep and long ago came thundering to the surface. "What kind of drugs?"

"OxyContin," he said, real low.

My ears rang, and the room suddenly felt ten times hotter. Danny only knew half the story about why I hated drugs. Everything that had happened with my sister returned to me, and my heart sank deeper into the pit of depression I'd been struggling against. Danny didn't know about her, but he knew about Ryan. That should have been enough.

"I tried to tell them it was a bad idea. And then, things got heated. I haven't seen Danny or Shelby since."

Is that why she'd been avoiding me? It was all making sense now. I took a large swallow of my drink. "Could I get a shot of Jose Cuervo?"

"Tamara." His mouth turned down at the edges. "Don't do this. This isn't you."

I laughed sardonically, twirling the straw around the glass. "You say that like you know me."

"I do." He smiled a sad smile, his gaze holding mine.

Yeah, right. He didn't even know my real age. *None of them* really knew me. Danny was always calling me his angel, but that wasn't who I was. That was his made-up version of me. Well, screw him and his ideals. "Sure ya do. Now, how about that shot?"

Charlie tilted his head to the side and tapped the bar.

"Coming right up." He put a shot glass in front of me and free poured. "Let me grab you a lime and salt."

I picked up the shot and slammed it down quickly. It burned going down my throat and warmed my belly. I chased it down with a drink of my iced tea.

Charlie's eyes grew wide. "That was hardcore."

"Like I said, you don't really know me." I pulled out a wad of cash. "I don't have a debit card, but I'd like to open a tab." I wasn't planning on leaving anytime soon.

My phone dinged, and I pulled it out to look at it.

It was a message from Danny, wondering when I'd be home.

Grabbing my drink, I ignored it and stood. I walked over to the jukebox and deposited a five-dollar bill.

That gave me thirteen songs to choose from. What was I in the mood for? Some Alanis Morissette man-hater music seemed appropriate. There had to be some good best-friend-betrayal music, too. My eyes landed on the song "Forgiven," and images of my sister battered my mind again.

I had played that song every night for a month after I abandoned Dakota and cried my eyes out. Would I ever be forgiven? Maybe what was going on with Danny and me was just another form of the punishment I deserved. Drugs and heartbreak would follow me wherever I ran too.

My phone dinged again. Another text from Danny.

`Tamara? Are you okay?`

I wanted to ignore him again, but if I didn't reply, he'd probably come looking for me.

`Ran into Milly right after work. We're down at Midway's with Charlie. Don't wait up.`

Hopefully, writing Charlie's name had made him sweat a bit.

Tears stung my eyes. As tough as I was trying to be right now, I wasn't very good at it. Every part of me just wanted to go home and curl up in Danny's arms. Why did life have to be this hard? Why did I always have to sacrifice myself for everyone else? What about what I needed?

I stared at my phone. Why hadn't Danny texted back? Why hadn't he said something sweet like he used to? Maybe it was time to finally leave this place for good. To leave Danny and Shelby too. Forget them both. Oh, that's right. No can do. All my savings went to buying a druggie a guitar.

I took a large swallow of my drink. *Was* he a druggie? Just because someone did OxyContin one time doesn't make them a druggie, does it? Maybe I was overreacting. I pressed D17 on the jukebox and Adele's "Set Fire to the Rain" came out of the speakers. Danny might not be a druggie, but his mood swings were killing me. And he *had* lied to me. Or at least, withheld the truth.

By the time Charlie closed down the bar, I was leaning over the counter, feeling the room sway back and forth. Charlie insisted he'd give me a ride home, for which I was grateful. I had told him I could walk home earlier that night, but at the moment, I didn't think I could make it to the door by myself.

Charlie gave the counter one more quick wipe and threw the rag in the bucket. "I have to give you credit. You tossed way more back than I thought you could."

"I used to drink a lot more than I do now." My words were slow and slurred.

He walked around the counter. "You ready?"

"As I'll ever be." I stood and immediately stumbled.

Charlie's arm came around my waist. "Whoa, girl. You just let me steady you. Put your arm around my shoulder."

I did what he said and he practically carried me out to his

car. "What am I going to do with you? Danny's going to kill me for over serving you."

"Screw Danny! I'm going to kill him for doing drugs!" I yelled.

"Shhh."

I laughed. "Don't 'shhh' me, Charlie. I'm going to literally kill him. I just need you to hold him down for me."

Charlie helped me into the front seat of his car. "Come on, Tamara. You know as well as I do that tomorrow, you'll be over this, and you'll love him again."

As drunk as I was and as much as I didn't want to agree with him, he was probably right. He pulled the seatbelt across my lap and made sure it was latched. The sweet gesture made me miss Danny.

It only took a minute and a half to get to Danny's house. Moving in with him had been a mistake. If I'd had my own place when he got into these epic funks, at least I'd have had a place to escape.

Charlie helped me up to the door and unlocked it for me with my key.

"Thank you," I said and gave him a big hug.

His eyes caught mine as I pulled away. "You take care of yourself, Tamara, and please don't tell him you know. He'll know I told you, and it could get real ugly." He pushed a stray lock of hair behind my ear.

"Remember a few months ago, when you told me you picked the wrong friend to hang out with that night?"

He nodded slowly, the energy between us changing.

"I think maybe I chose the wrong cousin. You're a real sweet guy, Charlie."

He smiled sadly and brought his hand up to my face, caressing the outline of my cheek. "I'm pretty sure that's the alcohol talking. We both know who you're in love with."

Standing on my toes, I kissed him on the cheek. "Maybe …"

"Goodnight, sweet girl." He kissed my forehead and then walked away.

As quietly as I could, I turned the door handle and crept inside. Danny had fallen asleep on the couch with the TV blaring. My heart hurt. That meant he was sleeping out here again. Which meant I'd be sleeping alone again. Why did I have to be so addicted to having his arms around me?

On the end table were his songbook and his cell phone. Something crept over me at the sight of his phone. Should I check it and see if there was any other evidence of drug use? It was a total invasion of privacy, but didn't I deserve to know the truth?

My feet seemed wobbly as I tiptoed toward it. Charlie *so* did over serve me. My heart jackhammered for two reasons as I picked up his phone. One, he could wake up and catch me. Two, the possibilities of what I might find.

I clicked on the message icon. The last person Danny had texted was Charlie.

`Better keep your mouth shut.`

That was right after his last message to me. Solid evidence that Charlie was telling the truth. Below the text to me was one from Shelby.

`I don't know if I can keep this up. I'm a terrible liar.`

And then, Danny's reply.

`You have to. She can't know about this.`

My heart broke. They sounded like the words of guilty

lovers. A loud sob erupted from my throat, and the phone slipped from my hands.

Danny bolted up off the couch just as the phone hit the floor.

December 9, 1:02 p.m. – Danny

"What do you mean, Tamara saw our text messages?" Shelby's eyes bore into mine almost as intensely as Tamara's had last night. "Why didn't you erase them immediately?"

One of these two women was bound to kill me, I was sure of it. I had played and now, the piper was calling in his dues. I just wasn't sure I had enough to pay him. "Don't act like this is entirely my fault. You're the one who initiated it both times."

"So, that's how it is? I'm the evil temptress ruining your life?" Her lips trembled as she spoke. "You're just like every other man in my life." She turned and grabbed the door handle.

I took her arm and pulled her toward me. "I'm sorry. I didn't mean that."

Her body was rigid. "I hate you right now."

"Listen to me. I care about you. This is an awful situation." I swallowed hard. There was no undoing the damage that we'd done. This was a proverbial time bomb. Sooner or later, it was going to explode and all three of us would carry wounds from it that would last a lifetime. "I smoothed it over for now."

"How?"

"I told her we were texting about planning her a surprise birthday party."

"That's right, her birthday is coming up." She looked up at

me, relief washing over her features. "And she believed you?"

"I don't know." I averted my eyes. Tamara had been in rough shape when she came home. When I told her about the party, a distant look had gathered in her eyes. "She didn't say much after I told her." I had picked her up and carried her to our room, where I'd held her for the rest of the night. The smell of alcohol had emanated from her. I hadn't expected for her to drink like she had. It scared me. But what scared me more was the betrayal I saw in her eyes.

The dream I had a few nights before I met her taunted me all through the night. My angel girl wasn't strong enough to save me. Instead, I was dragging her to hell with me.

Shelby's eyes were distant and sad. "We are the biggest jerks in the world. We need to come clean and let her go. If it happened only once, that's one thing, but there is more here, isn't there?"

She *did* have a good point. Shelby was better suited for me than Tamara. We deserved each other, and neither of us deserved Tamara.

December 9, 2:05 p.m. – Tamara

Charlie and I stood in front of the ocean with the wind beating against us. "What do you think I should do?" I said as my hair whipped around, flying in all directions.

He sighed and shook his head. "I wish there was an easy answer."

The conversation with Danny last night had been short and heartbreaking. As he spoke, I knew that he was lying to me, but I couldn't tell him without betraying Charlie. So, I quietly sat there like an invalid, letting him beat me with his lies. The consolation prize was that he held me for the rest of the night—something he hadn't done for weeks. And in that moment, I could feel that he did still love me.

He had shut himself away from me because of guilt. But wouldn't it have been better to come clean instead of keeping up with the lie? Knowing his story, I couldn't completely blame him. That was what he was taught by the person who was supposed to love him the most.

Charlie took my hand and pulled me around, so we were face-to-face. His eyes were sad. "How does a girl like you end up with a guy like Danny McMillan?"

A sad laugh escaped my lips. "Talent and looks," I said. And his sweetness and passion. There was actually very little that I didn't like about Danny. But there was a darkness in his soul that felt impossible to overcome.

Charlie gazed out into the ocean. "I hate to say it, but I still think the best answer is leaving this place. Shelby and Danny are toxic."

"That would be an option if I hadn't just spent all my savings on that guitar I bought him." I had started saving again, but it would take a while to build back up. Besides, there was no way I could leave either of them. I loved them both too much. They had become my family.

A gust of wind swirled around us, and I shivered.

Charlie pulled me closer to him, his body shielding me from the wind. The gesture felt friendly, as if he was trying to keep me warm. "Maybe I could help you with that."

I looked up at him, searching his eyes. Why was he set on me leaving town? Didn't he like having me around? "Is there something else you're not telling me?" Suddenly, it felt ten degrees colder.

"I just think you deserve better than being lied to."

Being lied to was awful, but maybe they were trying to protect me. They felt bad about doing drugs and didn't want to hurt me with it. "I need to get back to work. Thanks for meeting me, and for being there for me last night."

"Anytime you need me, I'll be here." He squeezed me tighter, kissed my forehead, and let me go.

January 3, 7:33 p.m. – Tamara

The holidays came and went without incident. Having a birthday so close to the holidays made it hard for me not to just lump Christmas, New Year's, and my birthday into one big celebratory mess. Unfortunately, I felt distant, as if I was just watching the holidays happen on a screen.

Danny had come out from behind his wall after the night I came home drunk. Things almost went back to the way they were before his birthday, except for the fact that I didn't see him the same way. As much as I tried not to think of it, there would always be a mark against him in my conscience. Danny did drugs with Shelby and instead of manning up and coming clean, he took the coward's way out and lied, again. It made me lose some respect for him, but it didn't make me stop loving him.

I didn't feel like celebrating my birthday, but Danny insisted I take the day off. He said he wanted to spoil me. He made me breakfast in bed and then surprised me with a spa-day package in which he was the masseuse. He had bought a huge basket of bubble bath, massage oils, and candles from Bath & Body Works, and lavished me with caresses and kisses. Maybe if every day was like that, things would actually end up being okay with us. What a fairytale that would be.

That evening, he said he was taking me to dinner at Mike's

Place, but when we passed it and turned onto Green Street, I knew we were going to Shelby's, to the surprise party they had used as a cover to lie to me. A part of me wanted to confront them. To let them know that I wasn't as stupid and naïve as they thought, but I figured it was better to let it go. The past was the past. Trust was broken. There was no way to get it back.

Danny pulled into Shelby's driveway and shut off the car.

"This doesn't look like the steakhouse you promised."

His mouth turned upwards into an impish smile. "The steak is inside."

"*Sure*, it is." My voice sounded a bit more irritated than I had wanted. "People aren't going to be jumping out at me, are they?"

He raised his hands in the air. "Anything is possible."

"I have really good reflexes. Someone might get punched."

"As long as it's not me." He exited the car, hurried around to my side, and opened my door. "My lady." He lifted his hand, motioning for me to get out.

His good spirits were nice. I decided to go with that emotion instead of the irritation I was feeling about being at Shelby's.

He took my hand and dragged me toward the house.

"Surprise!" A houseful of people yelled when I walked in the door. Had the whole town gathered for this ridiculous party?

There was only one person I wanted to see, and I was sure he wouldn't be here, after what he'd told me about Danny and Shelby.

"Chica!" Shelby ran to me and threw her arms around me. "Happy birthday." She pulled back, excitement radiating off her. "Do you know what this means? No more fake IDs, baby!"

I feigned a smile. "Right?" As if I even cared about that.

"Can you believe this turnout?"

I looked around the room. A lot of the people, I knew from

Bennett's. Some, I didn't know at all. "It's something else."

"Are you thirsty? We have plenty to drink." Shelby pulled me through the crowd of people to the island in the middle of her kitchen. There was every kind of alcohol imaginable. That would be perfect if it was *her* party, but for me, I would have liked something more low-key with a six-pack of beer and good music.

"What are you in the mood for?"

"I'll take a Coors Light, if you have one," I said to intentionally get on her nerves.

"Really?" She shot me a disapproving look.

I laughed. "How about a Lemon Drop?"

"*That's* what I'm talking about." She beamed from ear to ear.

"This is quite the party you've thrown together." I had to admit it was bigger than I expected.

"Danny and I have been planning it for weeks."

Those words were like a punch in the stomach. Had they done drugs again after that night?

I couldn't pretend any longer. "We need to talk."

Her baby blue eyes grew wide. "About?"

I grabbed her by the elbow and dragged her down the hallway to her room. "I know about everything." I pushed her down on her bed.

"What do you mean?" She fidgeted with the corner of the blanket.

"Don't lie to me, Shelby." I paced the length of the room before turning back to her.

She looked like an animal caught in a trap. "I don't know what you're talking about."

"I saw the text messages."

"You mean the ones about this party?" She was such a bad liar.

I glared at her. "Are we really going to pretend you haven't been lying to me since Danny's birthday? I *know*, Shelby."

"What did Danny tell you?"

"About the Oxy."

Something strange crept over her features. They became less tense, almost as if she was relieved. "We know how you feel about drugs. We didn't want to hurt you." She stood and put her arms around me, hugging me tighter than I had expected.

"It hurt worse that you kept it from me." I hugged her back. "And this party is absurd. Way too big. You and Danny know me better than this."

She laughed. "He put me in charge of the invitations."

"You're such a jerk." I pulled away from her.

Tears welled in her eyes. "I know, Tamara. I'm so sorry."

"I forgive you." I said. I could tell she was really broken up. I did forgive her for the drugs, but there was still this strange, nagging feeling that there was something she wasn't telling me. "Please don't tell Danny we had this conversation."

Her eyebrows flinched. "I won't. I barely even talk to him anymore."

I nodded, taking in her facial expressions.

She shifted her eyes. "Come on, let's go have fun and forget all this."

I stared at her, unsure. "Okay …"

"Come on, Tamara, it's your birthday." She grabbed me by my hand and pulled me into the kitchen, where she made me a Lemon Drop. I tried to enjoy the rest of the party, but it all seemed so fake. The other people weren't really my friends, and Shelby and Danny seemed to try too hard to ensure I was taken care of. Right after the cake and series of post-Christmas, low-budget gifts, my phone dinged.

`Sorry, I don't want to come in, but I'm out back. I`

have something for you.

A text from Charlie. I smiled, and it actually felt real. After playing nice with a room full of strangers, it would be good to see him. I looked around the room. Danny was deep in conversation with Bruce, a base player who loved music almost as much as he did. Shelby was with a group of people, playing quarters. They probably wouldn't even notice I was gone. I slipped out the back door.

Charlie stepped out from behind a large evergreen tree when he saw me.

My heart felt lighter as I walked toward him.

"Happy birthday, Tamara." His smile had a hint of sadness in it. "I brought you something." He pulled out a small, neatly-wrapped box.

"Oh, Charlie, you didn't have to do that."

"I know." He pushed the box toward me. "But I wanted to."

I took the gift, my eyes welling up. Why was I emotional all of a sudden? "That's really sweet."

"Open it."

Slowly, I peeled back the tape that was holding the package together. Once unwrapped, I lifted the lid off the black square box. Inside, there was an adjustable silver bracelet, with a charm dangling from it. I took a closer look. Two incised feathers encased a crystal-clear gem. On the back, it said "Godspeed."

I looked up at Charlie, giving him a confused glance. He motioned at the card inside. I brought it into the light.

The card read:

In Old English, "Godspeed" was the word one said to bless someone embarking on a journey. The expression bestows good fortune and safety, with God's grace.

I ran my fingers over the charm, feeling the outline of the feathers. Maybe it was time to spread my wings. Leave this place and never look back. To forget Danny and his depressive, self-destructive ways. And Shelby, too. Tears threatened to come again. Who was I kidding?

I finally made eye contact with Charlie.

He wore the same sad smile as before. "I know I've already said it, but I believe that you're strong enough to stand on your own."

The tears finally spilled over. He put his arms around me. His arms felt different than Danny's had lately. Pure and honest. Safe. Resting my head against his chest, I relaxed into his embrace. Why couldn't I have a guy like him? Warm, steady, attractive. Not stunningly attractive like Danny, but the adorable, guy-next-door kind of attractive.

He pulled back a little, his arms still around me. "You're such a wonderful person, Tamara. You have so much potential and worth. It kills me to see you selling yourself short by staying with Danny." He took in a deep breath, gazing into my eyes.

Then, my heart did something unexpected. It opened like a flower to the sun. After all the lying and distance from Danny, it felt good to hear someone being genuine. But what did he want from me?

"I love my cousin, but I firmly feel he is toxic for you, and so is Shelby."

His words hit me deep. More tears rolled down my cheeks. Charlie pulled me in close again, and I sobbed into his shoulder. I wished I could believe those words, but he didn't understand. Danny was the best thing life had given me so far. He wasn't perfect, but my heart wasn't ready to let him go. There was so much good in him. We could make it through a few missteps.

But maybe Charlie would be the safer bet for me. He

seemed to think the world of me, whether I deserved it or not. And his arms were tender and comforting.

I tried to talk through the sobs leaving my body. "I just don't know what to do. I know I was drunk when I said it the other night, but I'm completely sober now. Maybe I *did* choose the wrong family member."

"It's not like that, Tamara. Don't get me wrong, you're a beautiful woman inside and out, and I would be honored to be with you, but I don't think I'd be the best choice. There's too much twisted history between us. I don't think we could work."

What did he say? He did all this, and he didn't even want me. "I'm confused."

Charlie took a step back and wiped away more tears with the sleeve of his shirt, which now had multiple wet spots on it, smudged with mascara. "You can do anything you want to. That is the wonderful thing about life. You are a powerful person, and it is your choice. But if I could choose for you, I would choose for you to go and be free." He took the bracelet out of my hand and slid it onto my wrist. "Godspeed," he said under his breath.

"I really do love it." I ran my finger over the charm again, my head spinning from everything Charlie had just said.

"I have something else for you." He reached behind his back and pulled out a card.

I wiped my face with my hands and took the white envelope with my name on it.

"Please don't open it until you make the decision to leave. Whether that is tomorrow or ten years from now, it's your choice."

"Okay…" I stared at the envelope. Why didn't he want me to open it? Was there information in it that would make me want to leave town? I wanted to press him about it, but he'd been so kind to me over the last month. It was right for me to do what he'd asked. "Thank you, Charlie." I tucked the card in my back pocket and then slid my arms around his shoulders.

He embraced me back and there seemed to be an unspoken message in his touch. As if he was telling me goodbye.

January 17, 11:30 a.m. – Tamara

When I awoke, there was a strange foreboding weighing down my chest. I tried to wrestle with the feeling of dread, but as I showered and did my morning routine, the feeling built. I put on the bracelet Charlie had given me before walking out of the bathroom. Danny was lounging on the couch in his sweatpants, plucking at his twelve-string guitar.

He looked up at me, his chin-length dark hair falling over his sapphire eyes. "I'm writing this one for you, beautiful girl." I wanted to believe him, but after everything that had happened, his words felt false. Trepidation snaked its way along my spine as I leaned in to kiss him goodbye.

"I love you," he whispered.

"Love you, too," I said, but my stomach clenched. I was so sick of being lied to.

My fingers glided over the charm dangling from my bracelet. Was Charlie, right? Was it finally time to leave? Was this man in front of me just a shell of what I could have? I walked into our bedroom and reached into the back of the closet, where I had hid Charlie's card. In the background, Danny strummed lightly on his guitar. My eyes welled up at the thought of actually leaving him. There were so many things I'd miss. But was that worth everything else? Staring at the envelope,

Charlie's words played through my mind. *You can do anything you want to. But if I could choose for you, I would choose for you to go and be free.* I slipped the card into my purse and blew Danny a kiss as I walked by him to the door.

Freedom sounded like a wonderful idea.

January 17, 2:13 p.m. – Danny

There was a light tapping at the door. I gingerly placed the guitar back in the case before answering. Shelby stood in the doorway, her blonde locks swept into a high ponytail. Her blue eyes were lined with dark eyeshadow, her lips darkened with her usual red lipstick.

"Can we talk?" Her demeanor was soft, almost broken.

I stepped aside, so she could come in. "Of course."

Both of us had avoided each other at Tamara's party, but there wasn't a day that went by when I didn't think about everything and wonder how in the world I was going to fix this. Unfortunately, I saw no way around hurting Tamara. And hurting her like this would likely kill Shelby and me at the same time.

We couldn't go on acting, playing house—though I was becoming quite good at pretending. But continuing to live this charade was more than wrong. It was despicable. Tamara deserved a faithful man. One who was capable of holding her and cherishing her for the angel she was.

Shelby sat down on the couch and buried her head in her hands.

I took a spot next to her and placed my hand on her back, caressing her tight muscles.

She looked up at me, tears streaming down her face. "We have to tell her, don't we?"

Nodding, I swallowed back the lump forming in my throat.

"I don't want to lose her." Her lower lip trembled.

"Me neither, but it's the right thing to do. We can't keep pretending, Shelby. It's not fair to any of us."

"I know." She swept the tears off her cheeks. "Tonight, then?"

I nodded again.

"Can you do it?" She said, voice broken.

"Yeah, Shelby." I pulled her close to me. This was just awful. After everything Shelby had told me that last night we were together. She deserved better than this too.

"Thank you." She leaned into me, wrapping her arms around my neck. "What does this mean for us?"

"We just need to see how it all plays out tonight."

Moisture leaked from her eyes again. "So, if she chooses to forgive you, I lose both of you?"

"There's no good scenario here. We'll all lose something because of what we did."

"But you guys could end up making up, and then it's totally over for me."

I traced my fingers up her neck and then through her hair, cradling her head. "I don't want to hurt you like this."

Her lips met mine, lightly and sweetly. Her touch, like every other time, caused desire to pulse through my veins.

"Shelby," I whispered. "We shouldn't do this." Our gazes met, and I could see the raw desire in her eyes. Then her mouth was on mine again, and she was consuming every part of me like a wildfire.

"I want you so bad." She moaned. "One last time."

Standing, I took her hand and pulled her into my bedroom.

January 17, 2:16 p.m. – Tamara

Work was slow, which gave me too much time to dwell on the horrible feeling festering in my stomach. As I stared out at the ocean, thoughts hit me like the waves crashing against the beach. What if this feeling was like the nightmare I used to have about Ryan? What if this foreboding was telling me it was time to leave before Danny did something to really hurt me? What if Charlie was right? What if there was more for me somewhere else?

My stomach felt icy. All the times before, when I wanted to leave, it was to escape Ryan, but leaving someone that I loved because I thought it might be better for me felt selfish. Danny's mood swings were hard to deal with, but did that mean I should leave him? Maybe I could talk him into going to counseling.

When my boss sent me home almost four hours early, I thought about swinging by Midway's to talk to Charlie, but I already knew exactly what he would say. Just like every other time we talked, he would encourage me to leave. And just like every other time we'd talked, I'd draw the same conclusion. I couldn't leave. I'd built a life here in Ocean Shores. It wasn't a perfect life. But it was surrounded by people that I loved. Most nights, Danny's arms around me were enough to make me forget the other life I'd come from.

I drove past the bar and turned down our street.

When I walked into the house, something immediately felt off. Quietly, I latched the door behind me and inched my way toward the bedroom.

I opened the door, and there was Danny, naked, on top of Shelby.

Everything that I had built over the last year and a half crumbled into pieces in a split-second. "Are you kidding me?" I screamed. "Are you *effing-k*idding me?"

Danny jumped out of bed and threw on his pants, cursing under his breath.

Shelby snatched up her clothes and darted out of the room.

"You'd *better* run, you lying whore." I ran to the closet and grabbed my duffle bag. "So, this was it? This is what's been going on with you?" I opened my door and grabbed big handfuls of clothes, shoving them angrily into my bag.

"I'm so sorry, Tamara. I just—, I'm so sorry. You don't even know." The desperation in his voice sounded pathetic.

"I gave you *everything!*" I ran across the room and opened the closet door. "I hope you both rot in hell!"

"Tamara, I'm so sorry. We didn't mean for it to happen—it just happened."

I looked up at him for the first time.

Tears were streaming down his face, but it didn't faze me. I suddenly saw him for the pathetic low-life that he was.

"Moving in with you was the biggest mistake of my life. Oh, no, wait a second. *Loving* you was an even bigger mistake than that!"

I slung my purse and duffle bag over my shoulder. I ran out to my car and threw the bag in the backseat.

I drove out of there, my tires spinning out in the gravel driveway. In the rearview mirror, Danny was staring after me, his eyes beseeching.

As I drove out of town, I thought about the irony of it all. Staying in Ocean Shores had felt safe because of Danny, but he had hurt me far more than Ryan ever could. I would rather have died a thousand times at Ryan's hands than feel the deathblow that had just been dealt to my soul. I stamped on the accelerator. What Danny and Shelby had done to me would follow me forever.

For the longest time, I drove and cried and then cried some more. I had no idea where I was going or how I was going to survive once I got there. In my hurry to leave, I had forgotten my money jar in the corner of Danny's closet. As I pounded the steering wheel, a slew of curse words flew out of my mouth. I was so dumb to trust Danny and Shelby. Charlie had been right about both of them. God, why hadn't I listened to him?

When I hit I-5, I took the exit going south. My only option was to leave this awful state. Washington was no longer Washington in my mind. It was a land of empty promises and broken dreams. A land where my heart died.

As I gunned the accelerator, I noticed the gas tank was getting close to empty. Awesome. If I remembered correctly, I had about eighty dollars in my purse from the last couple days' worth of tips. That would at least get me out of the state, but that was about it. Depression weighed down every part of my body as I imagined sleeping in my car for the next few months, trying to get back on my feet as I nursed my broken heart back to life.

I took the next exit and found a gas station. I went to grab my wallet out of my purse when my hand slid over the card, I put inside it earlier. Charlie's card. Sadness gripped my heart. I hadn't even said goodbye to Charlie. The only good and kind person I'd met in so many years.

More tears slid down my face. At least I'd finally done what he had wanted me to do. Had he known about Danny and

Shelby? How long had it been going on? Nausea tightened my empty stomach. Some questions were better left unanswered.

I ripped the envelope open and pulled out the card.

On the front of it was a young girl bending over a cake, blowing out the candles. The words on the side of the picture said, "Hoping all your birthday wishes come true." I opened the card and ten one-hundred-dollar bills fell out. Shocked, I picked them up and read the note inside.

Tamara,

I just wanted you to know how much I really do care about you. I see you, Tamara. The way you treat people. The way you care. And I want you to know that you deserve nothing but the best. The other day, I looked up at the sky during a beautiful sunset, and it made me think of you. In that moment, I said a prayer for you. That's right; this goofy, messed-up bartender prayed for you. I know sometimes it's hard to believe, but God has a plan for you, Tamara, and it's better than you can imagine. If you're reading this, it means you decided to leave Ocean Shores. The thought makes me sad for myself but happy for you. Go someplace wonderful and start over fresh. I'll be praying for you on your journey. With all my heart, Charlie

P.S.—Don't try to give the money back. I won't accept it.

I laughed through the tears falling down my face. That was probably the sweetest thing anyone had ever done for me.

God has a plan? Those words … I hoped they were true because sometimes, I felt as if I'd experienced enough pain to last me ten lifetimes. If nothing else, Charlie's kindness meant I wouldn't be starving for the next month, and that I could make it further south before having to settle down.

And for the moment, that had to be enough.

Next in Series

Thank you for reading Ninety-Nine Reasons!

If you enjoyed it, continue the series with:

Ninety-Nine Signs

Made in the USA
Monee, IL
21 January 2021

56532999R10114